He couldn't count on Dave Royal, but he felt the preacher was dependable. He'd wait a little longer to make up his mind about Phil. One thing was certain, he thought. Three determined armed men inside the jail could hold off a lynch-crazy mob. The question was, would he be able to find two men to help him—men he could count on when the chips were down?

Solid citizens! He almost laughed when he said the words aloud. He wondered why he had ever thought of them in the first place. Men like Dave Royal were about as solid as butter on a hot day. Then for some reason his mind centered on Vince Trollinger, who should be a solid citizen but wasn't. He had told himself Trollinger was the man he should start with. This, he decided, was the time to start.

LEE
LEIGHTON
HANGING
AT PULPIT
ROCK

BALLANTINE BOOKS • NEW YORK

ISBN 0-345-28853-X

Manufactured in the United States of America

First Edition: July 1967
Fourth Printing: July 1980

First Canadian Printing: November 1967

HANGING
AT
PULPIT ROCK

CHAPTER 1

Deputy Johnny Jones stood in the street beside the sheriff, Hawk Fremont, and watched him examine the cinch, saw him give his big black a pat on the rump and then go back to check the packs on his mule. Not that anything was wrong. Whatever the sheriff did would be right, by his lights at least.

It was just that Fremont had to have something to do. His temper was always hooked to a short fuse. Right now it had almost burned down to the dynamite. He'd already wasted three minutes waiting for his fishing partner, Zero Moran, and Moran still wasn't in sight.

Fremont straightened and looked at Johnny. "What's the matter? You look like you've been drinking sour cream."

"I wish you weren't going," Johnny said.

"Aw, come off it," Fremont said. "I couldn't get away all summer to go fishing because I didn't have a deputy. Now it's September, I've got you, and I figger I've got a little vacation coming before snow flies."

"Sure you have," Johnny conceded. "I still wish you weren't going."

Fremont's brother Phil came out of the house with a bulging paper sack and handed it to the sheriff. He was seventeen, exactly half his brother's age, and as different from him as two members of the same family could be.

Hawk was big and tough and brutal, with an eagle-beak nose and a black mustache that curled up on the ends and a jutting chin. Phil was slender with fine features, a sensi-

7

tive boy who had grown up here in Pulpit Rock in the shadow of his big brother. It hadn't been easy, Johnny knew. In the month that he had packed the deputy's star, he had learned that it was never easy to walk in Hawk Fremont's shadow.

"Mrs. Bolger made some sandwiches for you," Phil said.

"Damn it, I told her I didn't want—" Fremont began.

"She heard you," Phil said, "but she couldn't get you to come in for dinner and she's worried about you getting hungry. She says it'll be a long time till you and Zero camp and fix your supper. Take 'em."

"I ain't doing no such thing," Fremont snapped. "When I tell my housekeeper I don't want sandwiches—"

"All right," Phil said patiently. "Mrs. Bolger and I know you're big and stout. You don't have to prove it to us. They're good sandwiches. She put deviled ham in some of 'em. Now take them and shut up."

It was a funny thing, Johnny thought. Pulpit Rock was a tough town, but Hawk Fremont had established the fact a long time ago that he was tougher. Everybody was afraid of him, everybody except his kid brother and his housekeeper, and nobody risked pushing him on anything, again with the exception of his brother and housekeeper. Johnny wasn't sure what it proved except that even a hard case like Hawk Fremont had a soft spot. He took the sack, glowering at Phil, then wheeled back to face Johnny.

"Now then, Deputy," Fremont said angrily, "why do you wish I wasn't going?"

He had no reason to be angry with Johnny, but he had to be angry with someone. Johnny knew it was simply a case of his being handy, and for a moment he wished he hadn't said anything. He was tempted to pass it off by saying he'd had a bad dream about what was going to happen, then decided to tell the truth.

"You've been sitting on a boiling pot for a long time," Johnny said bluntly. "All it'll take to boil over is for you to leave town."

"Oh hell," Fremont said in disgust. "I'll only be gone for three days. Nobody's gonna raise Cain just because I'm out of town. They all know I'll be back. If anyone gets ornery, remind 'em I'll be back. That'll take the starch out of 'em in a hurry."

"Besides, Johnny'll be on hand," Phil said.

"Yeah, sure," the sheriff agreed. "Just throw the first yahoo into the jug who gets ornery. Let him cool off till I get back."

Johnny didn't know that Fremont's neighbors, Mrs. Engel and her daughter Annie, were in the street until Mrs. Engel demanded, "Sheriff, what's going on?"

Fremont turned. "Oh, I didn't see you, Mrs. Engel. Have you been downtown?"

"Yes, I've been downtown," Mrs. Engel said, her gaze flicking from Fremont to the pack mule and back to Fremont. "I had to go to the bank." She jabbed a forefinger at the mule. "I suppose you're going prospecting?"

"No, I ain't," Fremont said. "I'm going fishing with Zero Moran if he ever gets here. If he doesn't, I'm going alone."

Johnny only half listened to the conversation because he was watching Annie. He knew she had a crush on Phil, affection which the boy did not return. Johnny didn't know how long she had felt that way, but as far as the girl was concerned, it had been serious ever since he'd come to town.

Now Johnny fought an impulse to laugh as he watched Annie sidle up to Phil and Phil ease away so the distance remained the same between them. Finally Annie stopped, but the adoring expression remained in her brown eyes.

"You can't leave town tonight," Mrs. Engel said angrily. "I had to take four hundred dollars out of the bank to loan to my brother who's coming tomorrow from Ouray. It's the only day he can be here, seeing as it's Sunday, and I'm going to have to guard all this money till he gets here." She shook her reticule in Fremont's face. "I'd rest easier if I knew you were in town."

"Johnny will be here," Fremont said. "Don't worry. If anything goes wrong, just holler for him."

"Holler for *him?*" Mrs. Engel looked at Johnny disdainfully. "I'll sit up and watch this money myself with a shotgun across my lap. If anyone tries to break into my house, he'll get a load of buckshot in his seat."

"I'll bet he will," Fremont agreed.

Mrs. Engel sniffed. "I don't know why a woman ever depends on a man. Come on, Annie."

But Annie wasn't ready to leave. She sidled toward Phil again as she said, "Could you come over this afternoon and help me with my geometry? You wouldn't have a bit of trouble with it, but I do."

"I can't," Phil said shortly. "I've got work to do at home."

"Aw, let it go," the sheriff said. "It won't hurt you to help Annie."

"I can't," Phil said, and looked back along the street. "Here comes Zero."

"It's about time," Fremont said.

"Phil, Mamma made a wild raspberry pie this morning. It's awful good." Annie was close enough to lay a hand gently on his arm. "You could have a piece while you're helping me with my geometry."

Phil jumped back when he felt her hand. "No. I can't come." He turned away from her and yelled, "Hurry up, Zero. Hawk's going to have a piece of your hide."

"I'm sorry, Hawk," Moran said as he reined up. "My wife's sick and the baby's got the colic. I guess I'd better not go."

"She'll be all right and so will your kid," Fremont said. "Now let's get moving. When I say three o'clock, I mean three o'clock."

"Come on, Annie," Mrs. Engel said. "Phil don't want to help you. If you wasn't blind, you could see that."

Mrs. Engel took the girl's hand firmly and led her along the walk past the Fremont house. Annie was crying, Johnny saw. He felt sorry for her. She was a pretty girl in a fragile kind of way, but she threw herself too much at Phil, who didn't, as far as Johnny knew, have any interest in girls.

Fremont was in the saddle, the mule's lead rope in his hand. Moran still hesitated, apparently pulled between his love for his sick wife and baby and his fear of Hawk Fremont.

"I tell you I'm worried about my wife," Moran said. "I can't go off—"

"You come on," Fremont said angrily. "Damn it, I'm not going to tell you again. Phil, have Mrs. Bolger go over and stay with Lizzie Moran. Zero, I've had this trip planned ever since Johnny got here, and I ain't gonna be done out of it now."

Fremont rode down the street. Phil said, "Mrs. Bolger is a good nurse, Zero. You go ahead. Have a good time and bring back a couple of foot-long cutthroats."

Moran was a knot-headed man with a mass of unruly red hair, a nubbin of a nose, and a multitude of freckles. Sometimes Johnny thought he wasn't very bright, but maybe it was because he jumped every time Hawk Fremont told him to do something. It was no secret in Pulpit Rock that there was some sort of illegal arrangement that concerned both men, but Johnny had heard only rumors of it.

Fremont was half a block away when Moran finally nodded and said, "I'll count on that, Phil," and spurred after the sheriff. When he caught up, Fremont handed him the sack of sandwiches.

Phil glanced at Johnny. "You're scared, but you've got no cause to be. You're bigger'n Hawk. It's my guess you can lick any drunk in town."

"I ain't exactly scared," Johnny said. "I'm big enough to lick a couple of drunks, and I can do it, but that's not the point. Hawk's way and my way are different. He bulls headlong into everybody except you and Mrs. Bolger and knocks 'em over. As long as I'm working for him, I've got to operate the same. I guess it just goes against my grain."

"I know," Phil said gravely. "If he treated me the way he does most folks, I'd have run away a long time ago, but he doesn't. I don't know why."

"Well, there's one thing about it," Johnny said. "I've got to crack a few heads tonight to stay on top of the lid, or the pot will boil over and take me and Hawk with it. He don't know it, but he'll have more trouble one of these days than he ever dreamed about."

"They hate him, don't they?" Phil asked. "Just about everybody in town hates him."

Johnny nodded. "That's right. They hate him enough to shoot him in the back, but they're afraid to try it because they might miss." He saw that Annie Engel was standing in front of her house watching Phil. He said in a low tone, "Why don't you just give up and go help Annie with her geometry?"

"I'll pick my own girl," Phil said stubbornly. "She's not going to pick me."

"You know, we've got a couple of hound dogs on the ranch," Johnny said. "Sometimes they'll sit and look at me or Pa with just about the same woebegone expression in their big brown eyes that Annie gets when she looks at you."

"Aw, cut it out," Phil said angrily. He whirled and stalked into the house.

The girl called to Phil before he reached the porch, but he acted as if he didn't hear and kept going. The screen slammed shut behind him a moment later. Only then did Annie give up and go into her house.

Trouble, Johnny thought as he walked slowly along the street to the courthouse a block away. It didn't make much difference whether you were good or bad. You could be as tough as Hawk Fremont or as yielding as Zero Moran, but you were still going to have trouble.

He glanced at the granite wall that made up the south side of the canyon. A tall point of rock that was flat on top rose a good fifty feet above the rim. It looked like a pulpit and so had been given the name Pulpit Rock, which, in turn, had been given to the town.

He smiled a little as the notion came to him that even solid rock had trouble. A geologist who had been in town a few weeks ago had climbed the cliff to examine Pulpit Rock and had returned to say that the granite was eroding around the base. One of these times the whole thing would break free and come roaring down the side of the canyon and smash a dozen houses to smithereens.

Of course nobody believed it enough to move out. In a way it was the same with Hawk Fremont. He went right ahead in his brutal, domineering way, refusing to believe that someday the heavens would fall on him.

Maybe the sheriff had anything coming that happened to him, but the trouble was, Johnny thought, that Hawk Fremont would take his deputy and his brother and Zero Moran and it was hard to tell who else along with him.

CHAPTER 2

The Escalante County courthouse stood in the middle of a block at the end of Main Street, a frame building surrounded by a weed-covered yard. A row of scraggly cottonwoods, half of them dead, lined the sidewalks along the front. The jail, a solid stone building, sat behind the courthouse.

For a moment Johnny stood in front of the jail staring at the courthouse. He thought that the unkempt appearance of the block was symbolic of the attitude of the Pulpit Rock people toward law enforcement. There were, of course, a few solid citizens: Doc Schuman; the preacher, Ed Allen; Judge Ben Herald; and possibly a few more; but you could count them on your fingers and toes, and the chances were you wouldn't have to use your toes.

He stepped inside and tossed his hat onto the desk. This was all the office that the sheriff had. One wall was nearly covered with reward dodgers. A gunrack hung from another wall. A coal stove in one corner was the only source of heat in the building and in cold weather was never enough for the cells.

A door opened into a small side room that held a cot. When there were any prisoners, Johnny slept on the cot. The rest of the time he slept and cooked his meals in a two-room cabin across the street. The cot was uncomfortable and he hated to sleep on it. At present the jail was empty, so, unless he arrested someone, he'd sleep in the cabin tonight.

He sat down in the swivel chair and cocked his feet on

the desk, something he would never do under normal circumstances. Hawk Fremont contended that if a lawman expected to be treated with respect, he had to be dignified, and this position was hardly a dignified one.

Johnny grinned as he thought about it. He rolled and lighted a cigarette, thinking that for three days he, Deputy Johnny Jones, would be the law in Pulpit Rock. The rest of today, all of Sunday, all of Monday, and Tuesday until Hawk Fremont got back, which would probably be late in the afternoon, he would be filling Fremont's shoes.

He could do it. All doubt was gone now that the time was here. He regretted saying anything to Fremont about wishing the sheriff weren't going. If he were sheriff, he'd go at the job of law enforcement from a different direction. He'd try to use the solid citizens to keep the tough element in line, and he'd start working on Vince Trollinger, who should be a solid citizen and wasn't.

Johnny glanced at his watch. Four o'clock. Time he was making his first round. Since he was filling Fremont's shoes, he'd be tough and brutal, and he'd bulldoze anyone who got in his way. The sooner everybody knew that, the better. Certainly it would be the height of stupidity to try to change anything in the three days he was acting sheriff.

He started toward Main Street, thinking about Vince Trollinger. As far as the problem of law and order in Pulpit Rock was concerned, Trollinger was the key man, a fact that Fremont either didn't know or consciously ignored. Fremont was not a fool, so it must be the latter.

Johnny could hear the pulsating beat of the stamp mill up the canyon from Pulpit Rock. That was Trollinger's mill. The Rose of Sharon mine on the steep slope of the canyon above the mill was Trollinger's. Half or more of the business buildings in Pulpit Rock belonged to Trollinger. All of the houses in the red-light district across the creek were Trollinger's.

Only the kiss of sheer good luck had made Vince Trollinger a rich man. Twenty years before, he had been prospecting along the creek, and in trying to climb out of the canyon, he had made the discovery that had been developed into the Rose of Sharon mine, one of the best properties in the San Juan.

Trollinger had secured financial backing from a Denver bank; he'd lived by the jungle law of claw and fang for so

14

long that he had developed an uncanny sixth sense which had led him to do the right thing at the right time.

He survived the Panic of 1893; he paid off the Denver bank; and he developed the Pulpit Rock town site, which had proved almost as profitable as the mine. Somehow he had maneuvered to keep the town from being incorporated. Since there was no town marshal, whatever law enforcement Pulpit Rock had came from the sheriff's office.

When Johnny reached the end of the business block, he saw two men break out of the Belle Union, the one in front yelling in terror, the other one bellowing in wild, drunken rage. Johnny recognized them at once. The one in the lead was Rolly Poe, a half-pint odd-job man who hung around the saloons cadging drinks when he wasn't working—which was most of the time. The one pursuing Poe was Clay Trollinger, Vince's hulking eighteen-year-old son.

Poe barely reached the middle of the street when young Trollinger caught him and knocked him down, then jumped on top of him and began beating him. By the time Johnny reached them, Poe was a cringing bloody mess. Several men had followed them out of the saloon, but no one attempted to interfere.

Johnny hauled Trollinger to his feet. "You're going to jail for disturbing the peace," he said.

Trollinger cursed and tried to hit him, but he was slow. Johnny ducked and grabbed Trollinger by a shoulder, whirling him around so his back was to him. He slammed his knee hard against Trollinger's butt, the blow staggering him and knocking him forward until he finally lost his balance and toppled over on his face.

Johnny wheeled back and helped Poe to his feet. "You all right, Rolly?"

The little man felt gingerly of his face. "I reckon so," he said. "Thanks for pulling him off. He was making hamburger out o' me."

"Get on home and wash up," Johnny said curtly. "And stay out of trouble."

"You bet I will," Poe said, and scurried away.

Johnny turned to young Trollinger, who was sitting up in the dust of the street. Clay wiped a hand across his face, leaving dirt streaks from one ear to the other. He said thickly, "Pa will kill you for this."

"Why don't you stomp your own snakes?" Johnny asked. "No sense letting your pa have all the fun."

When Trollinger didn't move or say anything, Johnny motioned for him to get up. "I said you were going to jail." Still Trollinger didn't move, and Johnny said, "Clay, if I have to make a good boy out of you, I'll do it. Now get on your feet and walk to the jail, or I'll beat the living hell out of you and then I'll carry you."

Trollinger got to his feet, casting a quick glance at the men on the boardwalk. Charlie Roundtree, who owned the Belle Union, was among them, and he was probably the one Clay Trollinger thought would interfere, but he made no move and remained silent. Trollinger took a long breath that was almost a sob, turned, and started toward the jail, his feet dragging every step.

The distance to the jail was little more than a block, but Johnny judged they spent a good five minutes walking that far. He opened the metal door between the cells and the office and motioned for Trollinger to go in.

Clay Trollinger didn't say a word until the cell door was closed and locked; then he gripped the bars and pressed his face against them. He said, "The sheriff goes fishing and leaves you in charge, so you've got to show everybody you're as tough and ornery as he is."

"That's about it," Johnny said. "Why were you beating Rolly up?"

"He kept begging for a drink and I told him to stop it, but he wouldn't," Trollinger said. "Before you leave, I've got something to tell you. Hawk Fremont ain't gonna be sheriff much longer. When he goes, you go. Now I'll tell you something else. You'll be lucky to get out of town alive."

Johnny left the jail, feeling nothing but contempt for Clay Trollinger. He had not finished high school. He worked in the office of the Rose of Sharon mine only when he wanted to. If he'd asked for the moon, his father would have given it to him if he could. Fremont usually looked the other way when young Trollinger got into trouble, but if the situation was so bad that he had to recognize it, he always turned Clay over to his father, and that, of course, meant no punishment at all.

Now, as he walked back to the business block, Johnny wondered what Vince Trollinger would do. He also wondered about Fremont. The sheriff would have to do something because Johnny had broken an unwritten law when he'd arrested Clay Trollinger.

When he reached the business block Johnny remembered Clay saying Fremont wouldn't be sheriff much longer. This might be the wild talk of a drunk, but on the other hand there might be more to it. Hawk Fremont had a year to go on his term, and it would take something definite and serious to remove him from office. Hating him and being afraid of him wasn't enough.

Johnny started making his round of the saloons, telling the bartenders to keep things under control, that he'd arrest any man for disturbing the peace just as soon as Hawk Fremont would. He purposely left the Belle Union to the last because Charlie Roundtree was the spokesman for all the men and women in Pulpit Rock who made their living from the sins of their fellow men.

He wasn't sure that Roundtree would tell him anything, but he intended to find out.

CHAPTER 3

The Belle Union was nearly empty when Johnny stepped through the swinging doors. The day shift had not come off work yet, so it would be another two hours or more before the crowd gathered. The place would be jumping from that time until after midnight.

Charlie Roundtree liked to brag that the elegant chandelier which hung from the center of the ceiling had cost him ten thousand dollars in Denver, and Johnny believed he was telling the truth. The mirrors, the long cherry-wood bar, the oil painting of the buxom nude that hung on the wall behind the bar, the furnishings in the back room: all were the best in camp and represented a considerable investment. It was understandable that Roundtree would not tolerate any roughhousing. If a fight started that his bartenders couldn't handle, he sent for Hawk Fremont immediately.

As Johnny crossed to the bar, he saw that the Lawler twins were sitting at a side table, two glasses and a bottle of whisky in front of them. They were big men who had earned a reputation as barroom brawlers. They spent more time in the Pulpit Rock jail than any other ten men in the county. This was one reason they hated Fremont with a murderous passion. The other reason was that they couldn't whip Fremont and they had tried at least half a dozen times.

Now they stared at Johnny, their expression insultingly contemptuous. He reached the bar and nodded at Latigo, the bartender, then moved on to the back, where Charlie Roundtree stood watching him, an expression of amusement on his face. Not once did the Lawlers take their eyes off Johnny. By the time he reached Roundtree, he was convinced that before the night was over he'd have a whack at trying to whip the Lawler twins.

"I see you've got a couple of gentlemen at that table," Johnny said, jerking his head toward the Lawlers.

The amusement fled from Roundtree's face. "It's stretching the truth to call them that," he said.

"I'd like to talk to you if you've got a few minutes," Johnny said.

"I've got more'n a few minutes," Roundtree said. "As a matter of fact, I want to talk to you. I figured you'd be around. If you hadn't come, I was going to send for you." He nodded at the door opening into the back room. "Go ahead. I'll bring the drinks. What will you have?"

"A beer," Johnny said, and went on into the back room.

The oak table seated six comfortably. The chairs, also of oak, had arms and padded backs and seats covered with gold cloth. The spittoons were polished so that a man could glimpse a distorted version of his face in the gleaming copper.

A framed sign on the wall stated in tall black letters: TEN DOLLARS FINE IF YOU MISS THE SPITTOON. Johnny grinned every time he read it. Common gossip in Pulpit Rock contended that since Hawk Fremont had become sheriff, Roundtree had never collected on his sign. He cheerfully admitted that he wanted it that way. He was, Johnny knew, inordinately proud of the high-pile gold-colored Brussels carpet that covered the floor.

Roundtree came in and closed the door. He placed one beer in front of Johnny, then went around to the opposite

18

side of the table and pulled a chair back and sat down. He was an average tall man, a little too plump, a little too soft, and his hair was always too perfectly in place, so perfectly in place that Johnny suspected he wore a wig.

In the month that Johnny had lived in Pulpit Rock, he had never seen Roundtree when he wasn't dressed immaculately in black trousers, a Prince Albert coat, a white silk shirt and string tie, with a gold chain across his vest, from which dangled an elk tooth. He was deadly at close range with the derringers that he carried, but he never let down his dignity enough to brawl with the customers. His bartenders were toughs, and he paid them to do whatever fighting had to be done.

For a moment Roundtree's black eyes stared at Johnny over the top of his beer glass, then he put the glass down and lighted a cigar. Even with the table between them, Johnny caught the odor that always emanated from the man. He guessed it was a combination of cologne and bay rum and the pomade Roundtree used on his hair. Johnny didn't like it, although he realized it was probably pleasant to the girls on the other side of the creek.

"I don't know what you wanted to see me about," Roundtree said finally, "but I can tell you what I wanted to see you about mighty quick, and it may terminate our conversation. Here it is in one sentence: You are a damn fool for handling young Trollinger the way you did."

Johnny sipped his beer, then set the glass down and reached into a vest pocket for tobacco and paper. He said, "Charlie, I haven't lived in this camp as long as you have. Fact is, I haven't lived here long at all. Life is some different than it is in the west end of Escalante County, where I grew up. There's a lot going on here I don't know about, but I've seen enough to be sure that what Pulpit Rock needs is a few more damn fools."

Roundtree laughed. "You might be right, Deputy. All right, I've had my say. Now what did you want to see me about?"

"I guess everybody knows or will know in a few hours that Hawk's out of town," Johnny said. "I've got a pretty fair notion about what will happen tonight. They'll be out to see how good a man I am, and I figure to show them, but I can't be everywhere at once, so I'd appreciate it if you'll do what you can to keep the lid on."

"I always do," Roundtree said. "Even when Hawk's in town. That all?"

"No." Johnny fished a match out of his vest pocket, then held it and stared at it, the unlighted cigarette dangling from his mouth. "Charlie, when I locked Clay Trollinger up, he said Hawk wasn't going to be sheriff much longer. What did he mean?"

For a moment Johnny thought Roundtree's face turned pale, that he was unduly agitated, then he wasn't sure whether he imagined it or not. In any case, the saloon man took his time answering. He finished his beer, then put his cigar back into his mouth and chewed on it.

"He was drunk," Roundtree said finally. "Forget it."

"No, he wasn't that drunk," Johnny said, "and I am not going to forget it."

"How did you happen to get appointed deputy?" Roundtree asked. "You're an innocent right out of the sagebrush. I thought at the time Hawk hired you that he was hard up for a deputy."

Anger began churning in Johnny, slowly at first and then, as he thought about what Roundtree had said, the anger blossomed until he began seeing flashes of red. This was the city-slicker attitude toward the country hick, which he had felt more than once since his arrival in Pulpit Rock, but he had never before had it stated to him so bluntly.

"Have I failed at the job yet?" Johnny asked with deceptive mildness.

"No, but you're bucking a stacked deck," Roundtree said. "Arresting Clay Trollinger is part of what I'm talking about. There are some things you can do in this town and some you can't, even if they need doing. This is an example."

"I'd do it again if I had it to do over," Johnny said. "I may be an innocent right out of the sagebrush, but I'd rather be that than cowards like most of you are. If you weren't cowards, you wouldn't be kissing the Trollinger butt the way you do."

"That's tough talk," Roundtree said, flushing.

"It's time for tough talk," Johnny snapped.

"Well, how did you get the appointment as deputy?"

Roundtree knew, Johnny thought, but he told him anyway. "It's been the custom for a long time in Escalante

County for the sheriff to come from the east end, where most of the people are, and he appoints a deputy from the west end, which is cattle country. When Frank Durwood resigned as deputy, Hawk asked me if I'd take the star."

"Why did you take it?" Roundtree asked. "Your dad is the biggest cowman in the county. You had a good job working on his JJ. Why come here and run the risks you do toting the star for a man like Hawk Fremont?"

"Two reasons," Johnny said. "Both good ones. I was tired of living at home and falling into a good job just because the outfit belonged to Pa. The other reason is that I'm engaged to Jan Prescott, and she moved here last spring. It's a hell of a long ride from the JJ to Pulpit Rock just to court a girl."

"I savvy that," Roundtree said, nodding, "but take some advice from a man who has been in business in this camp right from the day Vince Trollinger laid it out. Resign your job, Deputy. Get out of Pulpit Rock. Take your girl with you. Hawk Fremont deserves all the hell that's coming to him, but I don't think you do."

"Hawk's ornery and he runs over people," Johnny said. "Is that what you've got against him?"

"Hell no," Roundtree said angrily. "He's greedy and he's a bigger crook than the men he arrests and kicks around. He comes in here expecting free drinks. He plays poker at this very table when the rest of us don't want him and he knows it. If he loses, he's hell to get along with. He goes across the creek and expects to get what he wants from the girls free." The saloon man shook his head. "He's sheriff, Johnny, but he's not God. We're all dirt under his feet. He's got to go, one way or another."

"I take it that you haven't figured out how to get rid of him," Johnny said.

"We'll get the job done." Roundtree rose and added brusquely, "I'll expect you to drop in a few times tonight."

Johnny had no choice but to get to his feet too. He had not lighted his cigarette. Now he fired it and carefully deposited the match in the spittoon. He said, "Charlie, you haven't told me the whole story."

"I said you were an innocent," Roundtree said angrily. "You're stupid, too."

21

Roundtree walked to the window and stood there, giving Johnny his back. For a moment Johnny stared at him, then he shrugged his shoulders and left the room. As he strode the length of the saloon to the bat wings, he felt the eyes of the Lawler twins all the way to the door. Then he was outside, and he took a deep breath of the cool mountain air. He was glad to get out of the saloon, glad to get away from Charlie Roundtree, who made him feel like a callow youth.

He glanced at the sun, which was almost down, remembering that he was due for supper at Jan Prescott's. Slowly he walked to the end of the block and turned left toward the cabin that Jan occupied on the north bank of the creek.

A sour taste was in his mouth. He had been called an innocent from the sagebrush. He had been called stupid. Maybe, just maybe, Charlie Roundtree was right. If he was, Deputy Johnny Jones had better give up his star and go back to working cattle.

CHAPTER 4

Jan Prescott had grown up on a small ranch in the west end of Escalante County not far from the Jones spread, but there had been one major difference. Johnny's father had been successful; he had made enough money to enlarge his herd and buy several neighboring ranches, but Jan's father had been pursued by bad luck. He'd died the previous winter as poor a man as he'd been when he'd started his Rafter P twenty-five years ago.

Jan's mother died when Jan was twelve, and she had kept house for her father as long as he needed her. Johnny had begged her to marry him when her father died, but nine years of keeping house on the Rafter P had soured her. She'd had all the dirt and hard work and poverty of a cattle ranch she could take, so she sold out to Johnny's father and moved to Pulpit Rock.

Now, as Johnny approached Jan's cabin, he thought she had succeeded in escaping some of the dirt, or at least the red dust that was in the air most of the time in the arid west end of Escalante County. It rained more here in the mountains, and the ground held a rich carpet of grass and wild flowers. But she had not escaped the hard work or poverty. She had started a dressmaking business, but the only work she had found was for the girls across the creek, work she would have scorned last spring.

The front door was open, and Johnny could see Jan sewing on something even now with the light fading rapidly. He had told Charlie Roundtree the truth when he'd said he had come here to be near her. It was much more of the truth than the other reason he had given, that he was tired of living at home and working for his dad. As a matter of fact, he got along very well with Pete Jones, and he enjoyed working with cattle.

Ninety per cent of his reason for coming to Pulpit Rock was his necessity for seeing Jan often. He had been so used to spending Sundays with her and seeing her two or three times during the week that he couldn't stand it after she left the ranch. Now he stopped outside and looked at her for what must have been a full minute, thinking how much he loved her.

"Good evening, future Mrs. Jones," he said.

Jan jumped and stuck her finger with her needle and cried out, then she slammed the dress goods onto her cutting table. She rose as she said angrily, "John Jones, someday I am going to take my dullest scissors and cut your head off. Judge Ben Herald will call it justifiable homicide."

Johnny laughed as he stepped through the doorway. "He would, indeed, and give you a medal for getting rid of a pest to boot." He cupped a hand under her chin and tipped her head back. "Honey, when you're mad, you get color in your cheeks as bright as a scarlet bugler. That makes you mighty pretty."

The anger went out of her and she smiled. "You sneak up on me and scare me to death, and then you finagle and get around me. It happens every time."

"Oh, I'm a great finagler." He pointed to the blue velvet cloth that she had thrown down on the cutting table. "I thought you invited me for supper."

"Oh, I did." She ran the tips of her fingers over the cloth, her face turning grave. "Antoinette said she just had

23

to have this dress finished by tomorrow evening, so I was trying to get as much done on it as I could."

She was silent, her gaze on the cloth, but he had a feeling she wasn't thinking about it or Antoinette. In his eyes she was a very pretty girl with auburn hair and brown eyes and a pert nose, but that wasn't really important to him one way or another.

She was a spirited woman with strong feelings about what she liked and didn't like, and what she believed and didn't believe. He admired this trait, telling her that a woman who lacked it was like mashed potatoes without pepper or mince pie without brandy, and although it led to quarrels, their relationship was all the sweeter when they made up.

He studied her, puzzled. Something was out of place, and he couldn't put his finger on it. She seemed aloof and withdrawn, and he couldn't account for it because it wasn't like her. Jan Prescott was always a participant of life, never a spectator.

"How about supper?" he asked tentatively.

"It won't take long," she said. "I baked a chocolate cake this morning. I'll put the steaks on right now." She took a long breath and then she whirled to him and put her arms around him and hugged him. "Johnny, can we get married now? Tonight? Tomorrow?"

This wasn't like her, either. She always played coy when he came, making him work for his first kiss, but before he could answer, she tipped her head back and pulled his down so their lips met.

Johnny laughed softly when she drew away at last. "Oh, honey doll," he said. "You are as unpredictable as an April breeze. I've begged you to marry me so often that it's got monotonous to say it again. You always said no, we had to wait."

"I'm tired of waiting," she said wearily. "Tired of sewing and kowtowing to those terrible women. Well, I shouldn't say they are all terrible, but most of them are. I want to go home. I thought we could start a ranch of our own."

"Sure we can," he said. "The JJJ for Jan and Johnny Jones."

"Can we get married?" she asked eagerly. "Tomorrow? Or even tonight? I'd go off and leave this stuff if we could." She threw out a hand toward the dressmaker's dummy, the sewing machine, and the cutting table. "I'll let anybody have it who wants to come and take it."

"This is a queer experience for me," Johnny said, "but I'm the one who has to say wait awhile. I never thought I would."

"Wait for what?"

"For Hawk to get back. It'll be sometime Tuesday afternoon. As soon as he gets here, I'll turn in my star and we'll call in the preacher, and then we'll head for home."

"That may be too late. By that time you'll probably be dead." She turned away. "I guess I knew what you'd say. I'll start frying those steaks. I expect you're hungry."

He followed her into the kitchen. "Will you please tell me what you're talking about. Why will I be dead by Tuesday afternoon?"

"Sit down, Johnny." She went into the pantry and returned with the steaks. She started to pound them, then she stopped. "I'm sorry I didn't marry you last spring after Pa died. I've been sorry ever since, but I've been too stubborn to admit it. Now I feel like I'm standing on the bank of a stream and I'm watching a man drown, and I can't do a thing about it."

"Will you please tell me—"

"They'll murder you, Johnny," she cried. "You're too proud or too loyal or something to ride out of this awful town and let them kill each other off. That's what they deserve. Hawk Fremont ought to be killed. He's no good. He's a cruel, greedy, selfish man."

Johnny held his head. "I must be losing my mind. I keep asking you what this is all about, but all I get is more of the same thing. Now I'll try once more. Why will I be dead by Tuesday afternoon?"

"They're going to kill Fremont, and you'll try to arrest them, and then they'll kill you."

"How do you know all this?"

"I was in Antoinette's place yesterday when Charlie Roundtree came in with a couple of other saloon men and that gambler named Saul Moffat. They were in the bar and I was in the parlor, but they didn't know I was there. I had to wait to see Antoinette because she was busy upstairs, so I heard some of their talk. They said Fremont had been bleeding them too long and they were going to pay the Lawler twins to murder him."

"I guess I'm not surprised," Johnny said thoughtfully. "They don't want the lid held on as tight as it is, but Hawk's a hard man to kill."

"It's not a matter of holding the lid on," she said. "They all hate him, partly because he's so mean. Mary Lou is supposed to be his girl, but he never pays her anything, and if she isn't always ... well, enthusiastic about him, he beats her. I can't prove this, but I've heard rumors that he blackmails all of them and takes ten per cent of their profit. He told Mary Lou that if he stays here one more year, he'll have enough saved to live on the rest of his life."

Johnny stared at Jan, at first refusing to believe this, and then, thinking about Clay Trollinger and how Charlie Roundtree had refused to give him satisfactory answers to his questions, he decided she might be right. But he didn't say so. She was worrying enough as it was.

He told her about arresting Clay Trollinger and said he guessed he'd let him out of jail after supper, that Clay would have been in long enough by that time. He was silent as she dropped the steaks into a frying pan, then he said, "Don't worry about me, Jan. They won't do anything until Hawk gets back, and we'll pull out as soon as he does."

"Is that a promise?"

"It's a promise," he said.

He rolled a cigarette, wondering if he would be alive Tuesday afternoon when Hawk Fremont returned. If the murder scheme had gone as far as Jan said, it might have gone further, far enough to remove a deputy that Roundtree and the others knew they couldn't control.

CHAPTER 5

Vince Trollinger was a dreamer. He was also a rich man. The two facts were related. If he had not been a dreamer, he would not have spent years prospecting in the San Juan Mountains as he had, he would not have discovered the Rose of Sharon mine, he would not have borrowed every nickel he could and built the mill and borrowed again to develop the town site and even loaned money to men like Charlie Roundtree and Dave Royal, the banker.

Now, with the sun almost hidden behind the rims to the west, Trollinger put his feet on his desk and leaned back in his swivel chair. He had been lucky. Or smart. He preferred to think of it as the latter.

In either case, he had not been guilty of making a business mistake since he'd hit it lucky twenty years ago. Maybe he'd been lucky when he'd stumbled onto outcroppings that led him to the rich vein which had transformed him from an itinerant prospector to one of the richest and most important mine operators in the state of Colorado.

Now he faced a problem. He was the only one who could solve it. He had no one to turn to for advice, and he wouldn't have asked for advice if he'd had someone. One thing was sure. He could make a mistake very easily. He had a chance to sell the mine, the mill, and his town property, but he wasn't sure it was the thing to do.

Ted Riley, Trollinger's secretary, opened the door a crack and said, "I'm leaving now."

"All right, Ted," Trollinger said. "I'll lock up."

Riley closed the door. A moment later Trollinger heard him open and shut the street door. Funny how a man gets used to a routine, to an office, to the people he works with, to his home. He guessed that was why he hesitated. Logic pointed to one decision—sell.

If he sold, Vince Trollinger would have all the money a man could use in the years he had left. He would have enough, too, to work out some kind of trust fund for his son, Clay. He was dead sure of one thing. This would have to be set up carefully or Clay would have all the money spent in a month. He had put this off too long. He'd see Judge Ben Herald early Monday morning and get him started on it.

If he had any failure of which he was ashamed, it was the way Clay had turned out. He had not married until after he'd made his strike, then his wife had died when the boy was ten years old. With the help of a number of housekeepers, most of them far from adequate, he had spoiled the boy, giving him everything and anything he wanted. It had been the easiest way, and now that he saw it was the wrong way, it was too late to undo the damage.

He tried to avoid thinking of Clay. He guessed that was the real reason he considered selling. Oh, sure, the margin of profit had been going down steadily for several years, but that might change overnight. The next blast could lead into high-grade ore similar to what the Rose of Sharon had produced in previous years.

He took his feet off the desk, and flipping back the lid of his cigar box, took an expensive Havana cigar and fired it. He walked to the window and stared moodily into the street, puffing absent-mindedly.

Monday noon was the deadline to accept or reject the offer he was considering. It was a good offer, something over a million dollars. The buyers knew what was happening to the Rose of Sharon, but it didn't make any difference. Maybe the new men had a stock deal in mind. Or maybe they were gamblers and expected to find more high-grade ore.

He glanced at his watch. Just time for a drink in the Belle Union and then supper. He hadn't seen Clay all day, but Clay would be on hand when it was time to eat. The boy's talents were limited: eating, drinking, and spending money. That was it.

Trollinger clapped his black derby on his head and went out through the street door, locking it behind him. Now, honest with himself, he knew that the real advantage of selling out and leaving Pulpit Rock was the fact that he would not have to see Clay every day.

Maybe he would never see his son again if he left Pulpit Rock. It would be a relief. The only thing he could do was to fix up the trust fund so the boy wouldn't starve to death and then let him go to hell on a toboggan the way he wanted to. There wasn't a damn thing Vince Trollinger could do to stop him.

As he crossed the street, he wondered what Charlie Roundtree had done about getting rid of Hawk Fremont. Trollinger hated the sheriff. Fremont bowed and scraped around in front of him and let Clay raise hell and didn't do anything about it because his name was Trollinger, but the bowing and scraping were phony. The truth was, Fremont had only contempt for him.

There was nothing unusual about hating Hawk Fremont. Everybody did, except his brother and housekeeper and maybe Zero Moran. Perhaps Moran hated him, too. He had reason to, with Fremont shoving his nose into the dirt all the time. Oh yes, there was that cowboy deputy, Johnny Jones. Well, if he didn't hate Fremont now, he would, given a little more time.

Trollinger often wondered how Fremont managed to get elected. He guessed it was mostly because no one had the courage to run against him. He wondered, too, why the men who were trying to buy him out hated Fremont the way they did. They were Denver men, who had been here and had met Fremont. Something had happened, maybe in a poker game, or maybe in one of the houses across the creek, but whatever it was, the buyers were adamant about getting rid of Hawk Fremont before the deal was finished.

When Trollinger pushed through the bat wings of the Belle Union, he noticed the Lawler twins sitting at a table with a bottle of whisky in front of them. He nodded, but they didn't nod back. They sat and stared at him as if he were some kind of odd fish that by chance had stumbled into the saloon. This was typical of them, and it always made him furious.

He went on to the far end of the bar, where Charlie Roundtree stood toying with his elk-tooth charm. He said, "I've just got three minutes for a drink, then it'll be time to go home for supper. I suppose Clay's waiting for me now and faunching around because I'm not there."

Roundtree poured his drink, then he said, "I don't think so, Vince. The last I knew he was in jail."

"What?" Trollinger reached for the glass, then dropped his hand to his side. "Didn't Fremont go—"

"Sure he went," Roundtree said. "Right on schedule, with Zero Moran. Maybe he was a little late because he had to wait for Moran, but he's gone, all right. No, it was the deputy who arrested Clay."

Trollinger downed his drink and motioned for a second, something he never did. But this news was so staggering he had to find a crutch, and whisky was the quickest and surest crutch he could find. Hawk Fremont was a mean, cruel, dishonest son of a bitch if Trollinger had ever seen one, but at least he had enough sense to

29

know what the name Trollinger stood for in Pulpit Rock.

"I'll kill the bastard," Trollinger said. "What happened?"

Roundtree told him, and added, "It was the last thing I expected. I said to Jones just this afternoon he was crazy, but it didn't worry him."

"Well, I'll be damned," Trollinger said. "You know, I figured this Johnny Jones was just a kind of dummy Fremont hired to run errands for him, but he's got guts to do a thing like this. Even Fremont wouldn't do it. You think he'd do for sheriff? We're going to have to find somebody."

Roundtree shook his head. "We'll find somebody, but Jones won't do. I saw that this afternoon."

Trollinger turned the whisky glass with his fingers. He asked hesitantly, "What about Fremont?"

"He'll be taken care of," Roundtree said. "We found out from Moran where they were going."

Trollinger picked up the glass and gulped his drink, tossed a coin on the bar, and said, "I guess I'll be eating alone tonight." He nodded at Roundtree and left the saloon.

He threw his cigar away when he reached his house, still unable to believe that a cowboy who had not shown any particular talent as a lawman would actually arrest his son. But then Hawk Fremont was not a man who would permit his deputy to show any talent as long as he was in town.

He went into the house, hung his derby on the hall rack, and walked back to the kitchen. He said to his housekeeper, "You can serve supper any time, Maggie. Clay won't be here tonight."

"He's already here, Mr. Trollinger," the woman said. "He's in your study, I think."

Trollinger wheeled, strode back along the hall, and opened the door into his study. Clay was there, sitting at the desk in the swivel chair, one of his father's cigars tucked into a corner of his mouth.

"How'd you get out?" Trollinger demanded.

"Oh, you heard?" Clay asked.

"Charlie Roundtree. I asked how you got out."

"I guess Jones just got to feeling sorry for me," Clay answered. "Supper ready?"

Trollinger began to tremble. "You stupid fool! Why did you give that deputy an excuse to jail you?"

"I didn't think he would." Clay got up and dropped the half-smoked cigar into the spittoon at the end of the desk. He looked at his father, his bloodshot eyes turning ugly. "I'm broke. I need a hundred dollars and I need it now. Give it to me and I'll go to the hotel for my supper. You can eat in peace without the company of your stupid fool son."

This was the straw that broke the camel's back. Vince Trollinger's fists closed at his sides and he heard the heavy sound of his own breathing. He thought of the thousands of dollars he had given Clay in the last year, dollars that the boy had thrown away on women and whisky and poker, and he thought of his own boyhood with its hard work and privations. But there was something else over and above the anger that possessed him, the realization that as long as he kept playing Santa Claus, Clay would continue to be the parasite that he was.

"You'll eat here if you're eating," Trollinger said. "From now on, you're going to work for any money you get from me. I want you to show up at the mill at six o'clock Monday morning. I'll tell Mike Maloney to give you a job, something simple that you can do."

A pulse began hammering in Clay's forehead. "You're fooling, ain't you, Pa? You don't mean that? I'm supposed to work in the office."

"I mean it," Trollinger said. "I should have meant it and said it a long time ago. Now let's go eat."

"To hell with you," Clay raged. "I'll make you so damned sorry, you'll wish you'd never had me."

He stomped past Trollinger into the hall and out through the front door, slamming it behind him. Trollinger walked to the window and watched the boy until he turned the corner into Main Street. For the first time since his wife had died, he felt like crying. He had lost his son. No, he had lost him a long time ago, when he'd started giving him anything he asked for, but he hadn't known it then.

CHAPTER 6

Johnny released Clay Trollinger from jail, then went to the Fremont house. The relationship between Hawk and Philip was very strange, he thought. Hawk's love for his kid brother did not seem in keeping with his tough and callous nature.

Johnny knew he was treading on thin ice, and he didn't know how Philip would react, but he felt he had to ask Philip some questions. The boy could do nothing worse than refuse to answer. He tugged on the bell pull, trying to think how he would phrase what he had to say, but the right words just didn't come.

Philip opened the door, pleasure showing in his face when he saw who it was. "Come in, Johnny," he said. "If you haven't had supper, Mrs. Bolger will fix you something."

"I had supper with Jan," Johnny said as he stepped inside.

"Well, Mrs. Bolger's just doing the dishes, but there might be some coffee left," Philip said. "Let's go back into the kitchen and see. She baked a cake that's wallopin' good larrupin'. I know some of that's left."

"Thanks, but I had cake at Jan's." Johnny stopped in the doorway that led from the hall into the parlor and stared at Philip. "What did you say? I thought Mrs. Bolger was staying with Mrs. Moran and her baby."

"I don't know what's going on," Philip said. "All I know is that Mrs. Moran and her baby are not sick, so Mrs. Bolger came home and baked a cake."

Johnny went on into the front room, trying to sort this out so it made some kind of sense, but it didn't. Not any way he turned it to look at it. Finally he said, "I want to talk to Mrs. Bolger."

"Go right ahead," Philip said. "One thing Mrs. Bolger likes to do is to talk."

Johnny went through the dining room and on into the kitchen, where Mrs. Bolger was washing dishes. She was a big woman with a round, pleasant face and a body that flowed outward to threaten every seam of her dress. Hawk Fremont had hired her years ago when Philip was small. More credit went to her, Johnny thought, than to Hawk for raising Philip and making him a fine boy.

Mrs. Bolger glanced over her shoulder at Johnny. "I'll bet you're here to help me with the dishes, ain't you, Mr. Jones?"

"No, can't say I am," Johnny said. "I'm wondering about some things and thought you or Philip might help me out."

"I'll be glad to help you out," Mrs. Bolger said, "but I don't know much about anything. When a body spends her time cleaning house and washing and ironing and cooking three meals a day, she don't have much time left for gossiping." She giggled. "And I do love to gossip, Mr. Jones."

"First, why did Zero Moran say his wife was sick and the baby had colic if both of them are all right?" Johnny asked.

Mrs. Bolger took her hands out of the dishwater and dried them on a towel that hung back of the stove. She sat down on a kitchen chair that squeaked as her weight descended upon it.

"I thought you might be able to tell me," she said. "It was the queerest thing. I went over there right after the sheriff and Mr. Moran left town. Well, sir, the baby was sleeping as peaceful as you please, and Sally Moran was down on her hands and knees scrubbing the kitchen floor. Now I don't know if you've ever been around colicky babies, but I have, and I can tell you they don't sleep like that one was."

"What did she say?"

Mrs. Bolger snorted. "I couldn't get nothing out of her. She was skittish as a wild colt, but she wasn't sick, judging from the way she was working. All she'd say was that Zero didn't want to go on this trip with the sheriff. That was why he said what he did, but she wouldn't give me no reason for him not wanting to go."

She picked up the corner of her apron and wiped her face. "I tell you, Mr. Jones, there's something that smells rotten about it, 'cause the sheriff and Zero have been friends for years, and they always take a fishing trip sometime during the summer."

"Was she worried or scared?"

Mrs. Bolger nodded. "Yeah, I thought she was, though Sally ain't the scary kind. Not by a long shot. She wasn't real friendly, neither, not the way she usually is. Kind of acted like she wanted me to get out of her house and go home, so that's exactly what I done."

Philip had come in and stood by the stove watching Johnny. He was very slender, his thin face accentuated by a sharp nose. He was not strong, and Johnny had heard Hawk talk fretfully about him. "I'm going to have to send Phil to college," Hawk had said more than once. "Maybe he'd make a good teacher or lawyer or something, but he sure ain't gonna make his living busting heads the way I do."

Now Johnny glanced at him and looked away, still not finding the right words to say what he had come here to say. He asked, "You know where they went, Phil? Hawk told me they'd probably head up the South Fork. Did he tell you that?"

Philip nodded. "That's right. I think they aimed to make it as far as the beaver ponds tonight. Tomorrow they'll go on up to Mirror Lake."

Johnny cleared his throat. "I've got to ask you something that may make you mad. Both of you think a lot of Hawk, but it's no secret that you're about the only two people in Pulpit Rock who do."

"That's no secret at all," Philip said. "Some folks even hate me just because I'm Hawk's brother. It's got worse the last year or so." He stared at the floor, shifting his feet nervously. "The truth is, I hate him sometimes myself when I hear about the things he does. I don't know whether I can stay in school all year or not."

"Sure you can," Mrs. Bolger said. "Hawk promised to send you to college next fall."

"I know, I know," Philip said sourly. "But I don't think anybody, me or *anybody,* can live without friends, and I sure don't have any. I couldn't even get into the high school literary society last year."

"You've got me and Mr. Jones for friends," Mrs. Bolger said.

"And Annie Engel," Johnny added.

Philip looked at him indignantly. "She's one friend I can do without. If I looked at her twice, she'd have me married to her."

Johnny nodded, understanding how the boy felt. He said, "What I want to know is this: Have either one of you ever heard anything, gossip or what you think might be true, whether Hawk takes a percentage of other people's earnings?"

"He wouldn't do that," Philip said sharply. "He'll push people around and he can be so damned mean, you wonder why he doesn't bite himself, but he wouldn't take any graft. Or blackmail anybody."

Mrs. Bolger didn't say anything. She rose and went back to the stove and suddenly was very busy washing dishes. Johnny said, "Mrs. Bolger, you haven't answered me."

"I ain't going to, neither," Mrs. Bolger said, keeping her back to him.

He would make a mistake to press her, Johnny thought. Mrs. Bolger had her own brand of loyalty, and he doubted that anything could induce her to betray it, or even to say anything derogatory about Hawk Fremont. But her reluctance to answer was in itself an answer, so he shrugged and said, "All right," and left the kitchen.

Philip caught up with him before he reached the front door. "What's this all about?" the boy demanded. "Are they ganging up on Hawk?"

"Looks like they are," Johnny said, "but it's like trying to grab hold of a shadow." He stepped through the front door, then turned back. "Phil, I don't know what's going on, but I'm aiming to find out if I can. I think you'd better stay inside no matter what happens."

"I'm not planning to go anywhere," Philip said. "There's nowhere to go, and nobody to go with if there was."

"I'll see you tomorrow," Johnny said, and walked away.

He moved slowly through the twilight, thinking about what Mrs. Bolger had said regarding Mrs. Moran and the baby. One thing seemed certain. If Zero had tried to get out of going with Fremont by using a false excuse about a sick wife and baby, he must have had a very good reason to want to stay in town.

Then Johnny remembered Jan saying the Lawler twins had been hired to murder Hawk Fremont. He stopped on the sidewalk in front of the Engel home, his hands moving automatically to a vest pocket for the makings. He rolled and fired his cigarette, beginning to make a pattern out of the facts he had.

If the Lawlers planned to murder Fremont while he was on the fishing trip, then they or somebody else must have found out where Fremont and Moran were going. If Moran had sold that information, he wouldn't want to be with Fremont when the murder took place. He'd know that if he were a witness, the chances were he'd be murdered, too.

Johnny stood staring at the red sky to the west. There would be a full moon tonight, so a man could ride reasonably fast. He knew Hawk Fremont would not want to be warned. He had said repeatedly he would not be wet-nursed by anybody. If some hard-nosed killer wanted to shoot him in the back, he'd just have to do it. He was sure of one thing, Fremont always said. Nobody was going to shoot him from the front.

Well, he had to be warned whether he wanted to be or not, but Johnny couldn't leave town, and Philip didn't know the country well enough to take on the chore. Besides, he was a poor rider. Johnny thought of Rolly Poe, who owed him something. He wouldn't want to make the ride, but Johnny was of a mind to do some persuading if he had to.

He walked to the corner and made the turn along a side street to Poe's shack. His knock brought the little man to the door. He said, "Come in, Johnny. I ain't got anything in the house to drink, but—"

"I don't want a drink," Johnny said. "I've got a job for you. Seems that there's a scheme afoot to murder Hawk Fremont before he gets home from his fishing trip. I want you to go to the livery stable and rent a horse. Charge it to the county. You ride up the South Fork to the beaver ponds and tell him."

Poe backed away. "I ain't doing no such thing. It'll be dark in a little while . . ."

Johnny caught a fistful of his shirt and twisted it. "I wouldn't send you if *I* could go or if I knew of a man I could send. I don't. You owe me something for saving your hide today. Now either you go or I'll march you over to the Trollinger place and let Clay finish what he started."

Poe swallowed. "All right. I'll go."

"Good," Johnny said. "If you get cold feet and back out, I'll pick up where Clay Trollinger left off and finish the job."

He wheeled and strode toward Main Street. It was time to start his evening rounds. He had expected trouble, but not the kind he saw coming. The Bible said a man reaped what he sowed. Hawk Fremont was about to harvest a bountiful crop.

CHAPTER 7

Johnny moved up the south side of the street, dropped into the Palace and went on to Cassidy's Bar at the far end of the block, then he crossed the creek on the footbridge and walked along the front of the cribs and the houses until he reached Antoinette's place. He crossed the creek again and strode along E Street until he reached the intersection of E and Main Streets. He moved along the north side of Main, stopping briefly in the Belle Union.

He noticed that the Lawler twins were still sitting at that same table, but now the bottle was almost empty. If they were going to murder Hawk Fremont, it seemed strange they were in town. It also seemed strange that they were drinking. Maybe not, though, for they had the reputation of being hard drinkers. He would not have thought much about it if Jan hadn't told him about the plan to kill Fremont.

The Lawlers would probably be gone the next time he came around. But they weren't. They sat at the same table, this time with a full bottle in front of them. Johnny began to feel better. Jan's wild story was probably just a rumor, and the Lawlers would drink until they fell out of their chairs; then Charlie Roundtree would have his bartenders drag them into the alley, where they could sleep it off.

The miners were off work now and all the saloons were booming. Poker games were going full blast. Men crossed the creek. Others returned to the saloons. As Johnny made his third round, it seemed to him that the business block was making a racket like a hive of irritated bees.

Johnny was not doing anything different than Hawk Fremont had done thousands of times during the past ten years. In fact, Johnny had made this round himself on a number of occasions, often keeping Fremont company, sometimes by himself.

It was very seldom that anything happened which required his or Fremont's attention. Sometimes men got drunk enough or furious enough over their poker losses to exchange hot words. Occasionally the hot words led to blows. More often than not the bartenders separated the combatants before they inflicted any more damage on each other than a bloody nose or a black eye.

Fremont made it a principle never to interfere unless a situation was shaping up into what might be a killing. In the month Johnny had been in Pulpit Rock as deputy, there had not been a gun fight.

Fremont said it was a good thing for the miners to see him or his deputy at regular intervals during the evening just to be reminded that a lawman was around. They were used to having him make his rounds, and Johnny was well enough known by now so that he attracted little attention. Everyone would have been surprised if he hadn't made an appearance.

By ten o'clock Johnny knew this Saturday night was different. Not that anything had happened. It was just that he had a feeling something was going to happen. He was aware that this feeling might be a product of his imagination, but he didn't think so. If impending trouble had a smell, that smell was in his nostrils.

So far he had not stopped in any of the houses south of the creek, but now that it was after ten, he decided he should. Fremont always said that this was a matter of judgment. Unless he anticipated trouble, he left the women alone. Each house had a bouncer to throw drunks out, and it was better, the sheriff said, to let them handle their own trouble.

Johnny thought about this now, and as he moved slowly in front of the cribs, the feeling of trouble was so compelling that he had a quick look into each house.

He discovered that there were no poker games going tonight. As he visited the houses, he saw that only a few men were drinking in the bars. He was not detained until he reached Antoinette's place. When he glanced into her bar, one of the girls called his name and crossed the room to him.

"Antoinette wants to see you," the girl said. "Would you mind sitting down in the parlor? I'll get her."

"For about one minute," he said. "I can't stay."

"I'll tell her right away," the girl said, and ran up the stairs.

Johnny stepped into the parlor and sat down on one of the red-velvet-colored chairs. Sin paid very well, he thought, and wondered how well it paid Hawk Fremont. Then he wondered if Fremont would live long enough to enjoy his earnings.

Antoinette came into the parlor a moment later. She was a tall woman with well-padded breasts and buttocks. Her face was painted, her blond hair carefully curled, and her low-cut black dress had a thousand sequins that winked at him under the overhead lamp.

"Thank you for seeing me, Johnny," Antoinette said. "I know you're busy tonight with Hawk gone. I suppose trouble will break out any minute."

"It might," he said.

He was curious about her age, but he could not make an intelligent guess. She was somewhere between thirty and fifty, and that was as close as he could come. She had moved here from Cripple Creek and bought the place, then had sent for the girls. Beyond that he knew nothing about her except that she had the best business in town and Charlie Roundtree was her solid man, two facts which were very likely related.

"You're a sweet boy." Her full red lips curved into a smile, her green eyes moving speculatively up and down his tall, hard-muscled body. "I'd like to know you better, but we've never had a chance to get acquainted."

"If you're trying to drum up business——" he began.

"Not at all." She shook her head. "I know Jan and admire her, and I want to keep her friendship. I'm afraid I wouldn't if I had your business."

Suddenly he hated her. He hated her painted face and wondered what she looked like under that mask. Even more than he hated her, he hated what had happened to Jan since she had come to Pulpit Rock, having to please women like Antoinette in order to make a living.

"You wanted to see me?" he asked roughly, promising himself that the dress Jan was working on now would be the last.

"I have a question," Antoinette said, "and I thought I'd better get an answer before we have a whole night of your protection. How much is it costing us?"

He started to say something, then stopped as he realized the implication of her question. Instead, he asked, "You're paying Hawk whether he's in town or not?"

"That's right," she said, making no effort to hide the bitterness that was in her voice. "Ten per cent right off the top whether he gives us protection or not, and he sure as hell can't give it when he's out of town fishing."

"Then it's up to me," he said, "and my protection won't cost you anything."

He started toward the door, knowing he had been here too long, but she put out a hand and gripped his arm. "Wait, Johnny. I'm a little too old to believe in Santa Claus. Why doesn't it cost me anything?"

"The county pays me," he said.

"Oh hell," she said. "Nobody works for that, not even honest Deputy Johnny Jones."

"Then let's say Hawk will take care of me."

"Not if I know that bastard," she said, smiling. "He'll squeeze——"

"I have to go," he said as he jerked free of her grip and wheeled toward the door.

"No, Johnny." She lunged after him and caught his arm again. "Wait. Let me do something for you if your protection is free. I was sore because I thought you'd pile it on top of what Hawk is already charging, but if you're not, then the least I can do is not to charge you for one of the girls. You can have your choice. I promise you Jan will never know."

She was very close to him; he felt smothered by her. He had heard about her perfume that she considered exotic. Imported it from Paris, she said, and at great expense. Now the smell of it threatened to choke him, the mask of her painted face seemed to leer at him, and all he could think of was that she was doing her best to hold him here while he was being set up for something. He didn't know what it was, but he had no intention of being her pigeon.

He broke free of her and lunged out of the room. Her bouncer was a big Irishman named Tim Muldoon. Johnny heard Antoinette scream behind him; he saw Muldoon's square, freckled face loom in front of him, saw the huge hands reach for him. He hit Muldoon on the jaw, a driving right that caught him flush on the button and knocked him cold.

He rushed out of the house as a man ran toward him, calling, "Jones? Are you in there?" Then he must have recognized Johnny in the finger of light that fell through the open door, for he shouted, "Come on. Charlie needs you. The Lawlers are raising hell in the Belle Union."

It was Latigo, Charlie Roundtree's toughest bartender. As Johnny sprinted across the footbridge and raced along E Street past Jan's cabin, the thought came to him that this was a rigged deal, that Antoinette had planned to hold him until Roundtree had his trap ready to spring.

He had no time to worry about the kind of trap it was as he shouldered through the bat wings, his gun in his right hand. He saw Ed Lawler standing a few feet inside, his revolver pointed at one of the bartenders and Roundtree, who stood only a step away from the bartender.

Al Lawler was on top of Roundtree's expensive cherry-wood bar. He was yelling at the piano player to hit up a tune because he was going to dance a jig and to hell with Roundtree if he didn't like it.

Johnny acted instantly and effectively. His left arm went out and circled Ed Lawler's neck and squeezed, cutting off his breath, as he jabbed the gun into the man's back. He called, "Al, you're both under arrest. Drop your

41

gun and get off that bar and head for jail. I'm locking you both up for disturbing the peace."

There were at least fifty miners and townsmen in the saloon, but no one raised a hand or said a word. They gaped at him, wide-eyed. In the tense moment of silence that followed, Al Lawler looked so shocked that under other circumstances Johnny would have laughed.

Ed gurgled something and dropped his gun. Johnny couldn't see his face, but from the pressure he was putting on the man's throat, he guessed that Lawler's eyes were about to pop out of his head.

From where he stood behind the bar, Roundtree cried out, "Let 'em go, Johnny. Let 'em go. I'll drop the charges."

Johnny didn't relax his pressure on Ed Lawler's throat, and Al, looking at his brother's darkening face, got off the bar. He laid his gun down and started toward the door. Only then did Johnny ease the strangle hold he had on Ed's throat. He heard the wheezy intake of breath, the man wilting and then weaving as his knees threatened to buckle under him.

"Stay on your feet." Johnny jabbed the muzzle of his gun harder against Ed Lawler's back. "This gun is cocked. If anybody tries anything, it goes off and Ed's a dead man."

Johnny wasn't sure, but he thought Charlie Roundtree gave a surreptitious signal to someone in the back of the room. They went out of the saloon, Al Lawler leading by ten feet, Johnny and Ed keeping pace. The gun was still pressed hard against Ed's back, the pressure not slacking all the way to the jail.

Five minutes later the Lawlers were locked up in the big cell. Neither, Johnny saw, was drunk. They glared at him through the bars, then Al burst out, "By God, you would have killed him, wouldn't you?"

"I would," Johnny said. "Just like you aimed to kill me. Or maybe somebody else in the Belle Union was fixing to do it. I'm not sure how you had it rigged. Want to tell me about it?"

They turned their backs to him, Ed massaging his throat. Johnny wheeled away, thinking it was just as well he hadn't had time to think about it, because he couldn't have done any better than he had.

Now he thought he knew why the Lawlers were still in town. They'd been hired to kill him first and go after Hawk Fremont later. Then Charlie Roundtree and his bunch would be in the saddle, and Pulpit Rock would be their oyster.

He would probably never know exactly how the scheme had been planned, but it had misfired, maybe due to timing. He had left Antoinette's place sooner than the Lawlers had expected. Now that the plan had failed, the town would be quiet, he thought.

Tomorrow he'd have it out with Roundtree. Antoinette, too, maybe. He couldn't prove it, but he was convinced that both were into the scheme up to their necks and he was lucky to be alive.

He was right about the rest of the night being quiet. By two o'clock the saloons were empty and locked, and he was asleep on the cot in the little room just off the sheriff's office.

CHAPTER 8

Johnny woke with the first faint light of dawn touching the window in the small side room of the jail, where he slept. For a moment he lay motionless on the cot, wondering what had brought him out of the deep well of sleep. There must have been some noise that did not belong to a quiet Sunday morning.

For a time he lay on his back as if he were paralyzed, his body still drugged by sleep, but his mind conscious. Then it came again, the shrill sound of a woman screaming. He sat up at once, the paralysis gone, and tugged on his boots.

One of the Lawlers yelled from his cell, "Something's wrong, Jones. Get to hell out of bed and go see about it."

Johnny grabbed his gun belt from the back of the chair where he had hung it and ran outside. He buckled the belt around his waist as he raced toward the sound of the screams, wondering if they had anything to do with the

Lawlers or if they had awakened his prisoners as they had him.

He reached Hawk Fremont's house before he realized that the screams were coming from the Engel place next door. The light was strong enough for him to make out a white-clad figure standing in front of the house, but he was going through the gate before he recognized Annie.

Lights were showing in some of the neighbors' houses, windows were being flung open, and across the street from the Engel place the banker, Dave Royal, stepped through the front door, stuffing his shirttail inside his pants.

As Johnny crossed the yard, Annie stopped screaming long enough to take a breath. When he reached her, she started again, a high, shrill sound that threatened to break his eardrums. She was barefoot; she wore nothing except her nightgown, which had been torn down to her waist; and her hair, which hung down her back, was tangled as if she had just got out of bed.

Johnny put an arm around her and drew her to him as he said, "All right, Annie. I'm here. What is it?"

She kept screaming, not hearing him, not even knowing he was there, he thought. She was hysterical, her body tense, and she did not stop screaming until he slapped her sharply on the cheek; then she sucked in a long breath and began to cry.

Royal, crossing the street, called, "What happened?"

"I don't know," Johnny answered. "Can you tell me, Annie?"

She sniffled and choked, and finally blurted, "Mamma's been murdered."

For a few seconds Johnny didn't say anything. He stood motionless, still holding the girl, and then the thought came to him that she must have had a nightmare, or perhaps she was only pretending, hoping to make Philip feel sorry for her.

"Maybe you were mistaken," Johnny said. "Let's go into the house and see."

"No, no." For a little while she had relaxed, but now her body became tense again. "I can't look at her. I just can't."

Other people were in the street, most of them men. They moved slowly toward the Engel house, as if not certain they wanted any part of whatever had happened,

44

but still drawn by curiosity. A light showed next door in the window of the Fremont house. Johnny hesitated, thinking that if Mrs. Bolger was up, she would be of help, but if it was Philip, he'd better stay away.

Finally Johnny made up his mind. He called to Royal, "Dave, go next door and ask Mrs. Bolger to come over." Royal hesitated, as if he, too, did not want to get involved. This was typical of Pulpit Rock, Johnny thought angrily. Leave everything to Hawk Fremont or his deputy.

"Go on," Johnny said impatiently. "This girl needs a woman to look after her."

Royal wheeled away and pushed through the crowd that had gathered in front of the house. Johnny thought of sending someone for Jan, then decided to wait. Mrs. Bolger could do all that needed to be done if she would come, and he thought she would.

Two people came through the gate. He heard a woman ask, "Can I help, Mr. Jones?"

He saw it was the preacher's wife, Mrs. Allen. Her husband stood behind her, not pushing himself, but waiting to see if he could help. Johnny didn't know either of them well. He hesitated, then said, "Annie, Mrs. Allen is here. I want to go into the house."

Annie was still sniffling like a child who couldn't quite stop crying, but she was able to nod her head. Johnny pushed her toward Mrs. Allen, who put an arm around the girl as she said, "Let's sit down on the steps, Annie. We'll wait outside until Mr. Jones tells us what to do."

"Go get Doc Schuman, will you, Parson?" Johnny asked.

"Right away," Allen said, and turned and drove through the crowd, starting to run as soon as he was in the clear.

More people began edging into the yard. Irritated, Johnny said, "Stay outside the fence, all of you except Mrs. Allen." He saw Mrs. Bolger coming with Dave Royal and added, "Let Mrs. Bolger and Dave through."

He turned to the house, then stopped, thinking that he'd probably find Mrs. Engel murdered just as Annie had said, and knowing that he should not be alone when he investigated. If he were Hawk Fremont, he'd bull straight

45

ahead and people could believe what he said he found, but Johnny Jones wasn't Hawk Fremont.

When Mrs. Bolger and Royal reached him, he said, "She's hysterical, Mrs. Bolger. You and Mrs. Allen look after her. Dave, you come with me."

He didn't wait to see if Royal was willing to come or not. He moved past Annie and Mrs. Allen, who were sitting on the steps, crossed the porch, and went through the front door into the hall. He struck a match and lighted the hall lamp because the shades were pulled and the interior of the house was dark. He lifted the lamp out of the bracket, noticing that Royal had stopped in the doorway.

"Come on, Dave," Johnny said impatiently, and went into the front room, Royal following with the greatest reluctance.

Nothing was out of place here. He knew that Annie occupied the front bedroom; that Mrs. Engel had the back bedroom, which opened into the kitchen; and then he remembered that Mrs. Engel had mentioned taking four hundred dollars out of the bank. This could be robbery if she actually had been murdered, an act of violence that had probably not been intended.

He glanced again at Royal, who stood motionless in the hall doorway. "Damn it, Dave, I'm tired of telling you to come on," he said, his patience running out. "She's probably in the bedroom."

He went into the kitchen, watching to see that Royal was with him. The bedroom door was open. Royal said uneasily, "Johnny, nobody in town would murder Mrs. Engel. She didn't have any enemies. Maybe she committed suicide."

Johnny didn't stop. He went on across the kitchen and into the bedroom, and then he did stop, trembling so violently that he was afraid he'd drop the lamp before he could set it down on the bureau.

Behind him Royal gasped, "My God, she *is* dead."

Mrs. Engel lay on a rag rug beside the bed. She was on her side, her body curled grotesquely so that her knees were almost against her chin. The nightgown was pulled up to her waist. Blood was a brown mask covering most of her face and made a dark spot on the rug. She had been beaten savagely, her skull crushed by the blows.

Johnny stooped and felt for her pulse, but he found none. He had not expected to, for his first glance had told him she was dead.

He straightened and glanced quickly around the room, but her reticule was not in sight. He picked up the lamp and followed Royal, who had backed into the kitchen.

"She took four hundred dollars out of the bank yesterday," Johnny said. "Who was there when she got it? I mean, who besides you and Annie knew she had that money?"

"I . . . I . . ." Royal swallowed; his eyes seemed to be on the verge of popping out of his head. "Johnny, you think she was killed because of the money? Somebody tried to rob her and she fought with him?"

"That's the size of it," Johnny said.

He started to say that he and Philip Fremont knew Mrs. Engel had the money, but decided against mentioning it. Hawk Fremont knew, too. He could very well have told Zero Moran. It was no good to say the two men were out of town, because there was no way of proving they had stayed out. It was no good, either, to say he hadn't done it and he knew Philip wasn't the kind of boy who was capable of committing a brutal murder like this.

"I don't think anybody was in the bank when she got the money," Royal said after a thoughtful pause. "Are you suggesting I did it? Or Annie?"

"No," Johnny said, "but I am suggesting that somebody was in the bank or looked through the window and saw her get the money. Maybe it doesn't make any difference, though. She could have told a dozen people about it."

He heard someone come in. When he stepped into the front room, he saw that Mrs. Bolger had brought Annie into the house and had taken her into her own bedroom. A moment later Doc Schuman appeared in the hall doorway, his black bag in his hand.

"Is it true?" Schuman demanded. "Mrs. Engel has been murdered?"

Johnny nodded. "She's in the back bedroom. Look her over and tell me anything about it that might be important."

"I'm going home," Royal said. "I think I'm going to be sick."

Johnny nodded, thinking that the banker very likely

would be. His face was more green than white. Schuman hurried into the kitchen, picked up the lamp, and went on into the bedroom. Ed Allen, the preacher, came in and asked, "Is there anything I can do?"

"Not now," Johnny answered.

"My wife said she thought Mrs. Bolger could do more for Annie than she could," Allen said, "so she went home. We have small children, you know, and she thought she should be home looking after them, but we do want to help if we can."

"I'll let you know," Johnny said.

He saw Mrs. Bolger come into the room. As soon as Allen was gone, Johnny asked, "Did she tell you anything?"

Mrs. Bolger's face was white. "She sure did, but I can't believe it." She lowered herself to the love seat, her big body sagging. "No, I just can't believe it. She'd better tell you herself."

Johnny went into Annie's room. The girl had slipped on a robe. She lay on the rumpled bed, her eyes wide open. Johnny pulled up a chair so that he sat close to her and asked, "Can you tell me what happened?"

"I woke up," Annie said in a monotonous tone. "I heard Mamma yelling, 'You can't have it.' I don't know what time it was, but it wasn't daylight yet. At first I thought Mamma was having a nightmare. She does sometimes. I got out of bed and ran into the bedroom. I heard him hitting her before I got there. I grabbed him by an arm, but he kept hitting her on the head. She was on the floor. Then he turned around and grabbed at me and tore my nightgown. He didn't hit me, though. He shoved me away from him and ran out of the room. I guess he went out through the back door."

"Did you see who it was?"

"It was still awful dark," she said, "and he had a white sack over his head. Or maybe it was a pillowcase."

"You don't have any idea who it was?"

"Yes, I do. I know who it was."

Her chin was quivering; a pulse was pounding in her forehead. He leaned over her as he asked, "Who was it?"

"You don't want to know," she whispered, and closed her eyes.

"I've got to know," he said. "Tell me."

"It was . . . it was . . . ." She swallowed, and then she blurted, "Philip Fremont murdered my mother and stole our money. He had Mamma's reticule in his hand."

CHAPTER 9

For what seemed a long time Johnny didn't move or even breathe. The girl was lying. Some things simply could not be. Black wasn't white. Night wasn't day. Philip wasn't a murderer. Annie Engel was getting even with a boy who had refused to have anything to do with her, but that would be hard to prove.

"You don't believe me, do you?" Annie asked.

Johnny took a long breath at last. He said, "Let's say you were mistaken. You told me it was dark. You also said he had a white sack or pillowcase over his face."

"I still know who he was," she said stubbornly. "I recognized him from the way he talked. Besides, he knew we had the money. You heard Mamma tell it in front of Philip's house, and Philip was standing right there. Everybody knows he doesn't work and his brother doesn't give him much money."

"All that doesn't prove it was him," Johnny said. "A lot of other people, including me and you and Dave Royal, knew your mother had the money."

"Are you trying to accuse me of killing my own mother?" Annie whispered.

"No, but I am telling you that Philip was one of several people who knew about the money. Besides, she saw other folks Saturday afternoon and evening, and she could have told them. Isn't that right?"

"Yes." Slowly she turned her head so she could look at him. "I recognized his voice, too. I told you I grabbed him, and he said to let go. He said he didn't want to hurt me. Philip wouldn't, Mr. Jones. He wouldn't want to hurt me at all."

"No, I'm sure he wouldn't," Johnny said. "He wouldn't want to hurt your mother, either."

Annie turned her head back to its former position and

stared at the ceiling. She had lived with her dreams about Philip for a long time, but they had remained only dreams because he had rejected her repeatedly. Now, looking at the girl's pale, drawn face, Johnny was as certain as he had ever been certain of anything in his life that she was striking out at Philip, maybe for the purpose of making him notice her at last.

"But he did," Annie said finally. "He hurt Mamma awful bad."

"Annie, have you thought that your saying this may get Philip hung?" Johnny asked. "I don't think you want that to happen."

Her little hands fisted on both sides of her; her chin began to quiver; and she said, "He deserves to hang."

Johnny rose and left the bedroom. Mrs. Bolger still sat in the love seat. He dropped down beside her and said, "She's lying. The trouble is folks will believe it if they hear what she's saying. We've got to keep her from telling anyone. Maybe I can find the killer if I have some time, but I'm not likely to turn him up in the next five minutes."

Mrs. Bolger stared at the opposite wall, not moving even as much as a finger. If Johnny hadn't seen her blink her eyes occasionally, he would have thought she was paralyzed. He asked, "Did you hear me, Mrs. Bolger?"

"Yes," she said in a tone low enough so that Annie could not hear her. "I know some things you don't know, and it hurts me to tell you, but I guess I've got to. One is that I changed Hawk's bed after he left town and washed the sheets and the pillowcase. They wasn't dry last night, so I left them on the line. This morning the pillowcase was gone."

Mrs. Bolger swallowed. "That ain't the worst. Something woke me before daylight. I was kind of scared for a minute 'cause I heard somebody going down the stairs; then I figured it must be Philip, but I didn't have any idea why he'd be up prowling around in the dark. I laid there awhile, but I didn't hear him no more, so I got to worrying, thinking maybe it hadn't been him after all.

"Well, I got up and knocked on his door. He didn't answer, so I went in, and I seen his bed was empty. I got back into my bed, but I couldn't sleep for worrying about him. After while I heard Annie scream, and a little bit after that I heard Philip come back up the stairs and go into his room."

Johnny was as cold inside as if he had swallowed a cold stone that refused to get warm. He still did not accept even the possibility that Philip might have been the murderer, but he was aware that a combination of lies and fact—and he accepted what Mrs. Bolger said as fact—might be all it took to hang Philip.

"Don't tell that to anybody else for a while," Johnny said. "I'm going to look around, and I'll talk to Philip. I'll ask him why he was up at that time of night."

He rose as Doc Schuman came into the room and set his black bag on the stand in front of the love seat. "I examined her," he said, "and I went over the room just on the chance that I might find something you hadn't, because I knew you had other things on your mind. Besides, you were probably in a state of shock, finding the body in that condition."

He stopped and glanced at Johnny uneasily, as if afraid Johnny would be offended because he was playing detective when that wasn't his business. Johnny nodded and said, "Find anything?"

"No," Schuman answered. "Mrs. Engel was beaten to death by a piece of lead pipe or a gun barrel or something similar. It looks as if a few blows fell on her shoulders, but most of them were on her head. The killer got frantic after he knocked her cold, I suppose. Anyhow, I judge he hit her a good many times after she was dead. Oh, there is one thing you wouldn't have noticed. If we find the killer, we will find some scratches on his face. I discovered some skin under the fingernails of her right hand. I'd guess she got him a good one right down the side of his face."

Johnny thought about that a minute, then he asked, "What would you say about the blows, Doc? Were they the kind that only a strong man could give her?"

"You bet they were hard blows," Schuman said. "Her skull was caved in. Who else but a strong man would . . ." He stared at Johnny as if he could not believe what he thought Johnny was saying. "You don't think Annie did it?"

"No, I don't think that," Johnny said.

Schuman waited, as if thinking Johnny would go on with whatever was on his mind; but when Johnny remained silent, the doctor added, "It was what was missing from the room that interested me. Everybody in town, I guess, knew she took four hundred dollars out of the bank and took it home in her reticule. That's what was missing. The natural place for her to leave it would be in her bedroom. She's a meticulous housekeeper and not a woman to leave anything out of its proper place. I even went through the drawers in her bureau. It isn't there."

Johnny was only half listening. He was wondering how much he could count on Schuman's saying only a strong man could have killed Mrs. Engel. Philip was far from a strong man, but it would be hard, perhaps impossible, to prove that Philip was not strong enough to have delivered the fatal blows.

Johnny got up from the love seat. "Look in on Annie before you leave, Doc. Maybe you'd better give her something to calm her down and make her sleep. I'd like to keep people from seeing her today if I can. She's been hysterical for a while, so don't believe anything she tells you, and don't go around town telling any suspicions she has."

Johnny started toward the hall door, but Schuman caught him by an arm. "Wait a minute, Deputy. There's something here I don't savvy. If she knows who did it, or even thinks she knows—"

"She's wrong," Johnny said. "That's why I need some time. It could be a hell of a bad thing to let folks know she's accusing an innocent man."

"Damn it, she ought to know," Schuman said. "She saw him, didn't she? If she says somebody did it, then I'd figure you'd better arrest that somebody."

"That's my job, Doc," Johnny said. "This town is loaded with trouble. Passing out the word that an innocent man murdered Mrs. Engel is all it would take to blow things right out from under us. Believe me, Doc, I know what I'm talking about."

Johnny jerked free from the doctor's grasp and left the house. He hated to think how bad the situation would be if the rumor got around town that Philip had murdered Mrs. Engel. There would be lynch talk within an hour, and it would take time, probably too much time, to get Hawk Fremont back into town, if he would come at all. One alternative was to move Philip out of town, but Johnny hesitated to do that. It might be considered a confession of guilt.

As he stepped off the porch and started around the house, he saw that a crowd still lingered on the street. He was irritated because they were here out of curiosity, standing there waiting like a flock of buzzards. Doc Schuman was a gossipy little man, and Johnny had no real faith that Schuman would not repeat what Annie said. Of course the townspeople would claim Johnny was trying to protect Hawk Fremont's brother.

Johnny found nothing that could be called evidence until he reached the alley. There, in the dust close to the shed that stood on the back of the Engel lot, he found the missing reticule and a wadded-up pillowcase with eyeholes cut in it. It could have come off the line back of the Fremont house, but that didn't prove Philip had taken it.

Johnny opened the reticule and found that the money was gone, as he had known it would be. He stuffed the pillowcase and the reticule into his pocket and crossed to the Fremont yard. He knocked, and when no one answered, he opened the back door and went into the kitchen. He strode through the kitchen and on into the front room, calling, "Philip." Hearing no answer, he climbed the stairs and knocked on the door to Philip's room.

"Come in," the boy said.

Johnny opened the door and stepped into the room. Philip was sitting at the window. He looked around to see who it was, then shrugged and said, "Sit down, Johnny. What happened next door?"

Johnny sat on the edge of the bed, feeling the tug of suspicion for the first time; then he saw there were no scratches on the side of Philip's face. If Doc Schuman was right, Mrs. Engel had marked the killer so he could be identified.

"Mrs. Engel was robbed and murdered," Johnny said. "Annie was knocked down, but she wasn't really hurt."

"Who did it?"

"I don't know, but Annie says you did."

Philip took a long breath and shook his head. "I've seen something like this coming for a long time, Johnny. She told me yesterday afternoon that she would find a way to get even with me. Well, I guess she found it, all right.

She's a mean girl. I've seen it more than once. Mrs. Bolger can tell you."

"I didn't ask Mrs. Bolger about Annie being mean, but she did tell me you weren't in your room early this morning when it happened."

"That's right, but I didn't go into the Engel house. I couldn't sleep, so I went downstairs and I sat on the back steps for a while. I've been thinking about running away, and I'd just about decided to do it before Hawk came. I got up and went into the house when I heard a woman scream. It must have been Annie."

Philip hesitated, then he said, "You see, I saw a man run out of the back door of the Engel house and go across the yard to the alley. He had something white over his head. It wasn't light enough to see anything about him except that he looked like he was big. I came upstairs then. If you want to know why I didn't go over there and find out what happened, I'll tell you. You said for me to stay inside no matter what happened."

Johnny nodded. "I told you that, all right. I think it's a good thing you did stay here. I believe what you just said, but maybe the people in town won't if what Annie says gets out."

"No, they wouldn't believe me," Philip said bitterly. "If they thought they could get at Hawk by hanging me, they'd do it." He clenched his fists, his head lowered. "Maybe you'd like to know why I couldn't sleep and why I had decided to run away."

Johnny nodded again. "If you want to tell me."

"I guess you know without me telling you," the boy said. "Sometimes I think I hate Hawk as much as everybody else does." He looked up then. "Johnny, do you know what it is to be without friends, to have boys walk off when you come up to them? I got to thinking about what you'd heard. You know, Hawk taking bribes and all. Maybe it's true. Maybe it's part of the reason folks don't like me."

He rose, so restless he was jumpy. "Do you know what it is to have Hawk tell me I can't do this or I can't do that, as if I was ten years old? He won't let me work. He won't give me any money. He wants to do my thinking for me. My God, Johnny, my own shadow doesn't even belong to me."

54

"I know a little bit about how he is," Johnny said. "Don't forget I work for him, but it won't be much longer. I'm going to resign as soon as he gets back to town." He rose and walked to the door. "I don't have much to go on, so you'd better keep on staying in the house. You may be here alone all day. Mrs. Bolger is with Annie."

Philip stood at the window, his back to Johnny, acting as if he hadn't heard a word the deputy had said. As Johnny left the house, he wondered if Hawk Fremont had any idea what he had done to his brother.

As soon as Johnny got back to the jail, the Lawler boys started yelling for breakfast. He had no charge to hold them on except disorderly conduct. If he took a case like that to Judge Ben Herald, it would be thrown out immediately.

He unlocked the cell and told the Lawlers to rustle their own breakfast and to behave themselves. They rushed outside without saying a word and headed for the Belle Union.

Johnny sat down at the desk, and opening a drawer, dropped the reticule and pillowcase inside. He closed the drawer and rolled a cigarette.

He didn't have the slightest idea how to go about solving a murder. The only men in town who were above suspicion were the Lawler twins. That, he told himself grimly, left a lot of suspects.

CHAPTER 10

Vince Trollinger woke early, more from habit than need. He started to get up, then remembered it was Sunday morning and lay back and closed his eyes. He wasn't sure he could ever learn to enjoy a lazy life. He found too much pleasure in doing things.

Still, it would be wonderful to live one day at a time and not have any worries except how to spend the money he had in the bank. He wouldn't have any labor problems or the slightest concern about the vein in the Rose of Sharon petering out.

55

There was a lot of world to see outside of this south-western corner of Colorado, better food to eat than Maggie's cooking, better liquor to drink than Charlie Roundtree kept in stock, and better women than the cheap floozies a man could find across the creek.

Then, as always, he thought about Clay and how he had failed with the boy. Trollinger had never been able to face failure, and he couldn't now. He rose, the day turning sour. Hard to tell where Clay had spent the night, hard to tell what he had meant when he'd said he'd make his father wish he'd never had him.

Trollinger dressed, remembering there were two things he must do first thing Monday morning: wire Denver that he was accepting the offer for his property and see Judge Ben Herald about the trust fund for Clay. He didn't have any idea how a thing like that worked; he didn't know how much income a month would be fair to the boy or even how to give it to him. If he allowed one thousand dollars a month, Clay would have it spent the first week. What would he do the rest of the month?

That wasn't really the question, he thought as he went downstairs. He had never been any part philosopher, he had never been a moralist, and he had always lived with the notion that a man had to look out for Number One. Now he was uneasy over a question that kept nagging him, a question he could not put out of his mind. How much did a man owe a son who had gone to hell the way Clay had?

Maybe Judge Herald could give an answer. All Trollinger could think of was that it would be sheer heaven not to have to look at Clay and quarrel with him and hear about the latest batch of trouble he had got himself into.

Maggie was working at the stove when he went into the kitchen. He said, "Good morning, Maggie. Have we got any hot water?"

"Good morning, Mr. Trollinger." Maggie felt of the teakettle. "It's hot enough for a shave."

"That's all I want," he said, and picked up the kettle.

"Breakfast will be ready in about fifteen minutes," Maggie said.

"I'll be done by then," he said, and went into what he called the bathroom.

When Trollinger had built the house, he had planned to have a real bathroom with all the fixings to show everyone in Pulpit Rock that if you had enough money, you could live as well as the millionaires in Denver. He had the bathtub and a mirror and a white stand that held a pitcher and basin. That was all. He had never got around to having the work done. After his wife died, he had no incentive.

He took off his shirt and draped it across the side of the tub, then poured hot water into the basin and stropped his razor. He stared at his face for a time before he covered it with lather. Maybe he flattered himself, but he thought he looked younger than fifty. No gray in his hair, his stubble was tough and wiry and black, and he saw no deep wrinkles.

He began to shave, telling himself there must be women out there in that big world he had never seen who would enjoy helping him spend his money, women who would be fun to live with. His wife had been too sedate, too strait-laced to suit a man who had struck it rich the way he had.

Suddenly he wondered if his wife's attitude had any-thing to do with the way Clay had turned out. He cut him-self on his chin, and he said aloud, "God damn that kid." He wondered why he couldn't put the boy out of his mind and forget him, but he wasn't sure he could even if he were hundreds of miles from Clay.

When he finished shaving, he sprinkled bay rum into his hand and spread it on his face, fussing with the cut for a time before it quit bleeding. He put on his shirt, but-toned it, and then carried the teakettle back into the kitchen.

"Breakfast is ready, Mr. Trollinger," Maggie said.

He nodded and went into the dining room. He stopped, staring at Clay, who sat at the table. He said, "I didn't expect to see you this morning. You must have got hun-gry."

Usually Clay would have flung something back in an angry voice, but for some reason he seemed beaten down this morning. He held a white handkerchief against the left side of his face. This, too, was unusual. Many times he had come to the table dirty or bruised from a fight and not caring how he looked.

"Yeah, I got hungry," Clay said.

Trollinger sat down in his usual place. He asked, "What's the matter with your face?"

"I cut it shaving," Clay answered. "The damned razor must have a knick in it. I made a long stroke down the side of my face, and it scratched all the way."

Maggie brought a platter of bacon and flapjacks from the kitchen and poured the coffee; then she asked, "Did you hear about last night?"

"I just got up," Trollinger said. "How would I hear anything?"

"There was a lot of racket real early," Maggie said. "Maybe you wouldn't have heard it if your windows were down and you were asleep, but I had to . . . well, I was outside and I heard it."

Trollinger buttered a flapjack and reached for the syrup. "What kind of racket?" he asked, thinking it had probably been a dog fight. Maggie enjoyed getting excited about very minor incidents.

"It was Annie Engel screaming like she was in hysterics, and I guess she was," Maggie said. "That young Deputy Jones finally got her stopped. I reckon she had a right to have hysterics." Maggie paused dramatically, then added, "Her mother was murdered early this morning. Before daylight, it was."

Trollinger started pouring syrup and almost forgot to stop in time. The syrup flooded the flapjack and reached the edge of his plate before he tipped the pitcher back. "The hell," he said. "You sure?"

"Oh, I'm sure enough," Maggie said with relish. "I went right down there. At first nobody seemed to know what was going on; but purty soon Dave Royal, who went into the house with that young Deputy Jones, came out and went home. He looked sick—you know, kind of green around the edges. Didn't say a word to any of us. Purty soon his wife came out of their house, and she told us about it.

"They found Mrs. Engel lying on the floor beside her bed with blood all over. Her nightgown was hoisted up to her neck. Annie had been . . . had been attacked. Her nightgown was torn clean down to her . . . to her . . . well, it was torn, so it ain't no wonder she was having hysterics."

Trollinger started to eat, but he found it was an effort.

He shook his head. "I don't know what we're coming to, a thing like that happening in Pulpit Rock."

"That's just what I told Mrs. Royal," Maggie said. "That's exactly what I said. I wanted to stay longer, but I knowed you'd want your breakfast. I guess everybody in town heard that Mrs. Engel took a lot of money out of the bank yesterday. Four thousand dollars, I heard it was."

Clay finished his coffee and held his cup up. Maggie left the room and returned with the coffeepot. Someone knocked on the back door. Maggie hurried into the kitchen, opened the door, and stood talking on the porch for a long time.

"I'm sorry about last night," Clay said. "I didn't mean what I said. If you want me to go to work in the morning, I'll take a whack at it." He grinned. "It had better be easy though. I don't know what I can do."

"We'll find something," Trollinger said.

There was nothing, absolutely nothing, Clay could have said that would have surprised him more than this. He could not remember hearing Clay say he was sorry about anything, and for him to be willing to go to work was incredible.

Trollinger rose, and going into the study, opened his cigar box and took out a cigar. In a few minutes he would walk downtown to the Belle Union and have a drink with Charlie Roundtree. He was anxious to find out if Fremont had been taken care of as Roundtree had promised. Charlie might not know until later in the day, but the sooner Trollinger heard, the sooner he would feel easy about the sale of his property.

He sat down at his desk, puffing with relish on his cigar. Good cigars, good whisky, and good women: if a man had these three, he could enjoy living, but he had to make do with a good cigar. It wasn't enough, he told himself resentfully.

He glanced around the room with its dark wood paneling, the high-pile Brussels carpet, and the rows of books. He didn't know why he called this room the study except that someone had said that was the proper word. The truth was, he had never opened a single one of the books. His wife had liked to read, but after her death he doubted that any of them had been taken off the shelves except for dusting.

Suddenly restless, he rose and went into the hall and took his hat off the rack. No use staying at home. He'd have his drink in the Belle Union. After that? Well, maybe he'd get his horse and buggy from the livery stable and take a drive. For some reason life had suddenly become unbearable here in Pulpit Rock.

He had opened the front door and stepped through it when he heard Maggie calling, "Mr. Trollinger."

He stopped, irritated, thinking that she had some little household problem she could solve without his help. But he waited until she hurried along the hall to him.

"I was just talking to Mrs. Moffat," Maggie said. "She stayed at the Engel house until Doc Schuman came out, and she says that Annie Engel accuses young Fremont of killing her mother and . . . and attacking her. You know, the sheriff's brother. They live right there next to the Engels."

"Well," Trollinger said thoughtfully, "that is a surprise."

He left the house, walking slowly as he turned this over in his mind. He didn't know what would happen now, but he didn't like some of the prospects. Getting rid of a greedy, dishonest sheriff was one thing, but murdering and robbing a respectable woman and raping her daughter were messy crimes that gave a community a bad name.

The Denver men who wanted to buy him out wouldn't like this news. They seemed to think Pulpit Rock was a law-abiding community. Maybe he could get the deal closed before they heard what had happened. Now that it was too late, he wished he had accepted their offer last week.

CHAPTER 11

Johnny sat at the sheriff's desk for a long time. He thought about the murder and how a vindictive girl like Annie could bring more misery into the world than a dozen ordinary people. He remembered, too, what Philip had said, that if people thought they could get at Hawk Fremont by hanging his brother, they'd do it, not even thinking ahead to the time when Fremont would be back in town exacting revenge for Philip's murder.

Suddenly Johnny realized it was past breakfast time and he was hungry. He didn't feel like going to his cabin and building a fire and cooking his own breakfast. He might just as well spend his money. He'd be marrying Jan and leaving Pulpit Rock in another two or three days. There had been a time when he thought he wanted to live in town. Now he knew better. He'd be glad to get back to the JJ.

He put on his hat and stepped out of the office into the warm morning sunshine. When he reached the business block, he was surprised at the number of men who stood in little groups on Main Street. Usually no one was out this early on Sunday morning. Then he heard the church bell and realized it wasn't as early as he had thought. Sunday School would be starting before long.

When he reached the Bon Ton restaurant, he paused on the boardwalk, his gaze moving from one knot of men to another. Most of them were townsmen, but some were miners. They glanced at him covertly, none of them speaking or even acting as if they knew who he was.

Johnny was not normally an overly imaginative or suspicious man, but he told himself there was so much hate in these men that he could feel it. He had the strange sensation of being in another town, because there was a sort of unreality about the whole scene. Even the silence wasn't natural.

The men were talking, but in low tones. No saddle horses or teams with rigs were tied at the hitch poles. He couldn't see or hear a dog; no chickens were in sight, although usually a dozen or more were scratching in the horse manure on the street. It was as if time had stopped and everyone was waiting for it to start again so something could happen that was part of the destiny of Pulpit Rock.

Turning, he went into the restaurant and nodded at Jake Norton, who, with his wife, ran the place and put out the best food in town. Norton gave Johnny a short nod back and stood waiting for his order.

No one else was in the restaurant, but Johnny reminded himself that it was Sunday morning. The good people were headed for Sunday School and church; the bad people were sleeping after dissipating most of the night. In this way he tried to assure himself that everything was perfectly normal, but he could not. The truth was, nothing was normal, not even for Sunday morning.

"Bacon and eggs, sunny-side up," Johnny said as he sat down on one of the stools. "Fetch me some coffee pronto. Your coffee will open my eyes if anything does."

Norton went back into the kitchen, gave his wife the order, and returned with a steaming cup of black coffee. He set the cup down in front of Johnny and leaned forward, palms flat on the counter. He asked, "You got the Fremont kid locked up yet?"

Johnny stared at the man for half a minute, his anger rising so quickly and sharply that he couldn't say a word for that length of time, then he said softly, "By God, I'll kill that doctor for shooting off his mouth."

"No, you won't," Norton said. "You'll do your duty and arrest that kid as soon as you eat your breakfast. What's more, if you want to save your own hide, you'll keep him in the jug until he's tried."

"Jake, believe me," Johnny said, "Phil did not murder Mrs. Engel. When I find out who did, I'll arrest him regardless of who it is."

Jake Norton was a tall, thin man, his face pasty white because he was seldom outside in the sunlight. Now his narrow lips tightened against his teeth, his eyes narrowed, his breathing sounded as if he'd just come in from a hard run.

"Johnny, I think you're an honest boy," Norton said, "and it's probably too bad Hawk Fremont talked you into leaving your job and taking the star, because Hawk Fremont is a mean, greedy son of a bitch who's had this camp buffaloed for years. Of course that's got nothing to do with this, but if you don't arrest the Fremont kid, folks are going to say you're afraid of Hawk. They might be right, too."

Mrs. Norton called from the kitchen that Johnny's breakfast was ready. Norton plodded back along the counter, returning a moment later with the plate of bacon and eggs. He set it in front of Johnny, then stepped back, his hands jammed into his pockets. Johnny ate rapidly, wanting to get out of the restaurant.

Norton was silent until Johnny had finished and had

tossed a coin on the counter. Then he said, "For your own sake, put the kid in jail. He'll be lynched if you don't, and his blood will be on your head. We can't and won't permit a boy who has murdered one woman and raped a girl to stay free to do it to my wife or your fiancée or some other decent woman."

Johnny had started toward the door, thinking that both Norton and he would be better off if he just walked off and stopped the whole argument. Now he turned and faced the restaurant man, asking, "Where did you get this rape business?"

Norton shrugged. "Doc didn't say she was raped, but her nightgown was torn. If he didn't rape her, he must have grabbed her, intending to do it, then got scared and ran."

"Whoever murdered Annie's mother did not rape Annie," Johnny said. "If you're any kind of a solid citizen, you'll set that rumor straight the next time you hear it. Now I'll tell you once more. Philip Fremont did not murder Mrs. Engel, and I am not saying that because I'm afraid of Hawk."

"The girl named him," Norton yelled. "That's good enough for me."

Johnny wheeled and stomped out, knowing he would say too much if he stayed. This was what he would have to buck all day. Tomorrow, too, if Hawk did not get back. He hoped Rolly Poe had found the sheriff and persuaded him to return to Pulpit Rock, but knowing how stubborn Fremont was, he had no confidence in that happening.

He paused on the boardwalk long enough to roll and fire a cigarette, and again he felt the eyes of every man on the street. They were judging him just as Jake Norton had judged, he thought angrily, deciding that Phil was guilty and that Johnny was not arresting him because he was afraid of Hawk Fremont.

Again he was aware of the silence, the immobility of these men who were staring at him. He moved past them to the corner, ignoring them and realizing he was seeing a new side of Pulpit Rock.

He had not considered seriously the danger to himself and Phil. Yes, the thought of a lynch mob going after Phil had been in his mind, but now it was more than a thought.

Sooner or later it would be certain to happen if Phil was not in jail and if Hawk Fremont stayed out of town.

Johnny rounded the corner and went along the side street, wondering if it would satisfy these men if he did arrest Phil or would their blood lust drive them to break into jail and lynch him? Hawk Fremont would be sore when he came back and found his brother in jail, but Johnny would face that situation when the time came. One thing was sure. Phil would be easier to protect if he were locked up in jail.

Johnny reached the church. Glancing at it, he saw Dave Royal standing in front talking to Ed Allen. Royal must have recovered from the nervousness that had plagued him earlier that morning. He looked all right now.

On impulse Johnny turned and climbed the steps. When he reached the door, he said, "I want to talk to both of you."

"I'm afraid we don't have time," Royal said, backing away. "We're late getting started now."

"You'll be a little later," Johnny said sharply. "I was in the Bon Ton just now and Jake Norton threatened me. He told me I had to arrest Philip Fremont to keep him from being lynched. To save my own hide, too. Have you heard this kind of talk?"

"Didn't I do enough for you this morning?" Royal asked. "Have you got to keep dragging me into your affairs?"

"What's happened is not just *my* affairs," Johnny said, the smoldering anger stirring in him again. "It's yours and Ed's and Doc's and everybody else's who considers himself a solid citizen. How do you consider yourself, Dave?"

Royal would have wheeled and gone into the church if Allen had not gripped his arm. "We are solid citizens, Johnny," the preacher said. "I have a notion that right now Pulpit Rock needs us, because something is happening, though I'm not sure exactly what it is."

"That's right," Johnny said. "Something *is* happening. That's why I stopped to talk to you. I'm going to need some help before this is over. Charlie Roundtree's bunch has run this camp too long, partly because Hawk Fremont has let them run it. I guess Hawk got paid pretty well to look the other way at times, but it's partly because you solid citizens have let it happen. Now I'm asking you again. Have you heard this talk about Phil?"

"Yes," Allen said. "I guess it's not my business to try to tell you yours, but since the girl has accused young Fremont, it seems to me you have to arrest him. If you do, it should satisfy the men who are doing the talking. If you don't, I'm afraid there will be a lynching, and that is the last thing we want."

Royal seemed to have found his courage again. He nodded and said, "That's right. You've got to put the boy in jail. He may be innocent. The girl may be mistaken. If so, he should not be afraid of a trial."

"One more thing," Johnny said. "If I do arrest him, it will be to protect him, not because I think he's guilty. Can I count on your help if there is an attempt to break him out of jail to hang him?"

"You can count on me," Allen said.

Royal nodded, his eyes not meeting Johnny's. "Sure," he mumbled. "You can count on me."

"Good," Johnny said, and turning, went back down the steps to the street.

He couldn't count on Dave Royal, but he felt the preacher was dependable. He'd wait a little longer to make up his mind about Phil. One thing was certain, he thought. Three determined armed men inside the jail could hold off a lynch-crazy mob. The question was, would he be able to find two men to help him, men he could count on when the chips were down?

Solid citizens! He almost laughed when he said the words aloud. He wondered why he had ever thought of them in the first place. Men like Dave Royal were about as solid as butter on a hot day; then for some reason his mind centered on Vince Trollinger, who should be a solid citizen and wasn't. He had told himself Trollinger was the man he should start with. This, he decided, was the time to start.

CHAPTER 12

As could be expected, the Trollinger house was the finest in Pulpit Rock. It was a two-story structure with a mansard roof. It was painted white with green trim, and was surrounded by a picket fence, also painted white.

Johnny had heard that the pane of clear glass in the front door was circled by small colored panes, and a man could look through one of these and turn the whole world blue or red or yellow. But Johnny didn't have a chance to experiment. He met Trollinger on the boardwalk, half a block from his house.

"Good morning, Mr. Trollinger," Johnny said. "I'd like to talk to you."

Trollinger stopped and looked at Johnny as if having trouble remembering who he was; then he said, "Oh, I suppose you're the acting sheriff now that Fremont's out of town."

"That's right," Johnny said. "You've heard about the murder?"

Trollinger nodded. "I presume you have young Fremont in custody?"

Johnny swore under his breath. The speed with which the grapevine dispatched a message from one end of Pulpit Rock to the other was astonishing and would beat any telegraph in existence. He said, "No. He didn't kill Mrs. Engel."

"Why, I understood that the girl named him."

"She did, but she was mistaken. It was dark in the

house, and the murderer wore a pillowcase over his head. She couldn't possibly have identified him."

"Then why did she name him?"

Johnny hesitated, wondering if he should tell Trollinger that Annie was taking revenge on a boy who had rejected her. He decided against it, thinking that Trollinger probably wouldn't believe him and he certainly would not understand.

"I suppose she was just mistaken," Johnny said. "That's what I wanted to see you about. There's some talk about lynching Phil. It may be only a wild threat, but—"

"It strikes me that the talk is justified," Trollinger interrupted. "If you're afraid to arrest the boy because of what Fremont will do when he gets back, I am of the opinion that a lynch party is in order."

In the month that Johnny had worn the star, he'd had almost nothing to do with Vince Trollinger. He had seen the man in the Belle Union a number of times, but he had not exchanged a dozen words with him in his life. He had heard a good deal about him from Fremont and Jan and other people; he knew that Trollinger's thinking centered around himself and his son Clay, and from all reports he didn't give a thin damn about anyone else.

Still, for him to stand here on the street and talk so lightly about a lynch party was too much. "I've got something to tell you, Trollinger," Johnny said hotly. "You have the most to lose of anyone in camp if we aren't able to keep law and order. You own the mill and the mine and half the town, including the best house, and if a mob gets out of hand and starts burning and looting, you'll be sorry you ever said a lynch party was justified."

Trollinger drew his shoulders back. He was not a big man, although he had a way of making himself appear big. He did have muscular shoulders and thick arms that had been toughened in his younger days by use of a pick and shovel, but his wealth and easy living had not softened him.

Now Trollinger glared at Johnny, anger smoldering in him. No one called him "Trollinger." It was always "Mr. Trollinger," or with a few poker intimates such as Charlie Roundtree and Saul Moffat, he was "Vince."

"You're a fool, Jones," Trollinger said in a belittling voice. "I don't know why Fremont hired you in the first place, but he did, and now if his brother has committed a crime, he should be arrested and held for trial."

Trollinger started to walk away, but Johnny gripped his arm. "You listen to me. I tell you I know Phil did not do it. If I arrest him, it will be to protect him, not because I think he had anything to do with Mrs. Engel's murder. I expected some help from you, some backing to help me keep the peace. A few words from you would do it."

Trollinger jerked free of Johnny's grip, his face turning red. "If you ever lay a hand on me again, Jones, I will personally cut you down to half your size. And don't expect me to do your work for you."

This time when he strode away, Johnny made no effort to hold him. He stared at Trollinger's broad back, thinking how easy it was to hate the man. He was not at all like Dave Royal and some of the others, who had no backbone. No, he was more like Hawk Fremont, arrogant, bursting with self-importance, and running over with smug superiority.

Johnny turned toward the Engel house, thinking that Hawk Fremont would be destroyed in one way or another before long, but the Vince Trollingers of the world, rich and powerful and disdainful of the law, would go on forever. Or would they? Maybe the Charlie Roundtrees would survive after the Vince Trollingers were destroyed; maybe the Roundtrees in their subtle and devious ways could shape and wrap the Trollingers to suit their purposes.

As Johnny walked up the path to the front door of the Engel house and tugged on the bell pull, he wished he had never taken the star but had stayed on the JJ, riding for his dad. But he had taken the star, he had a job to do, and he stood alone.

Mrs. Bolger opened the door. "Oh, it's you, Mr. Jones. Come in." She wiped her eyes with a wadded-up handkerchief that she gripped in her right hand. "I never felt worse in all my born days. Everybody says they're going to hang Phil. Maybe he did do it like Annie says, but he's got a right to a fair trial the same as anyone else."

"No, he didn't do it," Johnny said. "The trouble is, I don't have the slightest notion who did. Annie is lying to make trouble for Phil. I thought maybe I could talk to her and make her see what she's doing."

"You can't talk to her now," Mrs. Bolger said. "The doctor gave her something to make her sleep. It won't wear off until afternoon."

"I'll come back later," he said. "If I can get her to sign a statement that she lied, and if she will give me a description of the man who did it, I might be able to do something."

"Are you going to arrest Phil?"

"I haven't decided, but if I do, it will be because I think it's the only way to protect him and not because I think he committed any crime." He turned away, then called back, "If she comes out of it sooner than you expect, let me know. I'll probably be at the jail."

"I will," Mrs. Bolger promised.

Johnny walked away, wondering if he should stop at the Fremont house and talk to Phil. The boy was probably still in his room thinking about running away. If he did, it would be a confession of guilt to everyone in town and make it impossible for Johnny to avoid locking him up.

When Johnny reached the gate in front of the Fremont house, he decided to wait. Phil would be all right until dark. There would be no lynch party until then, and he didn't think Phil would try to run away while it was still daylight. He went on to the jail and there found Rolly Poe waiting for him.

"You find Hawk?" Johnny asked.

"Yeah, I found him." Poe swallowed. "He wouldn't listen. He just laughed in my face and said there wasn't a man in Escalante County who had the guts to try to kill him."

"You're going back to see him again," Johnny said. "Tell him that Mrs. Engel has been murdered and there's gossip that Annie was raped. Folks think Phil done it, and I may have to take him into protective custody."

"The hell." Poe wiped a hand across his face, staring at Johnny as if this were more than he could believe; then his lips tightened against his teeth. "No, I ain't gonna do it, Johnny. I'm tired and I'm hungry and I need a drink. What's more, Hawk Fremont is a genuwine son of a bitch."

"Take that horse to the stable and have Jasper give you a fresh one," Johnny said. "Go to the Bon Ton and buy yourself a good dinner, then start out. I need Hawk. You tell him to get back here pronto. Phil's life is more important than any fish he'll catch."

Poe groaned. "Ain't there nobody else you can send?"

"Nobody," Johnny said. "Don't make me start threatening you again. If I have to twist your scrawny neck—"

"All right, all right," Poe said. "I'll go."

Johnny watched him ride away, thinking that in the eyes of most people in Pulpit Rock, Rolly Poe was nothing but a barfly, but the way Johnny saw it, he was a better man than Vince Trollinger or Charlie Roundtree, or even Dave Royal.

CHAPTER 13

Johnny cooked dinner in his cabin, then returned to the jail. He was surprised to find Doc Schuman, Dave Royal, Ed Allen, and Judge Ben Herald waiting for him.

"Well, this is a surprise," Johnny said as he sat down at the desk. "It looks like a committee of solid citizens."

"We're not very solid," Herald said. "I've been out of town and just got back about an hour ago. From what I hear, somebody has been raising hell and propping it up with a chunk."

Johnny leaned back and rolled a cigarette. He said, "Somebody has for a fact."

An uneasy silence followed as Johnny lighted his cigarette and dropped the charred match into the spittoon at the end of the desk. He wondered if he could count on Judge Herald any more than he could count on Dave Royal and Doc Schuman.

Herald was an old man, probably over seventy, but he was vigorous and he had a mind of his own, even though he had come here to practice law not long after Trollinger had made his strike and Charlie Roundtree had started the Belle Union. As far as Johnny knew, he had never bucked either man openly, but he didn't think that proved anything. The old judge wasn't weak-kneed like Dave Royal and most of the other businessmen.

70

"We're here to ask you to do your duty," Doc Schuman said brusquely. "We want you to put Philip Fremont in jail, and we think you should have done it first thing this morning. Now the day is more than half gone, and he's still free."

Johnny pinned his gaze on the doctor, his cigarette dangling from one corner of his mouth, the smoke making a shifting shadow in front of his face. He wanted to throttle the man, to slap his round, pink cheeks until they were raw.

When he was able to speak, Johnny said in a low voice, "By God, Doc, of all the men in this camp, you have less room to talk about me doing my duty than anyone."

"Now wait a minute, Johnny," the judge said. "You've got more of a problem than you think you have. I stopped in the Belle Union for a drink just before I came here. It was crowded and the talk was ugly. I've heard the same kind of talk before. I can recognize the sounds, and I can sense the feeling among men that makes a lynch mob. It'll just take a spark of some kind to get it off, and you'll have a hundred yelling, half-drunk men heading for the Fremont house with a rope to hang Phil."

"I haven't been in the Belle Union today," Johnny admitted, "but I have talked a little bit, and I was on the street early this morning. I got the smell of it even then. I believe you, Judge, but do you know why this is happening?"

"Of course." Herald nodded his shaggy head. "We've got a little world of our own, made up largely of men. We have only a few good women. Mrs. Engel was one and Annie is another. One was murdered and robbed, the other one was raped. I can think of no other crime, unless it is molesting a child, that will arouse men like what happened this morning."

"Sure," Johnny said impatiently, "only Annie wasn't raped. Now tell him, Doc. Tell him what you did that I told you not to do."

But the doctor was not to be intimidated. "I don't even have to begin to defend myself, and I sure don't have to do what you tell me to, Deputy." He turned to Herald. "What he means, Judge, is that Annie said it was Philip Fremont who did the killing. He ordered me not to tell anybody. I told people what Annie said, and I don't see any reason yet why I shouldn't have told them."

"Damn it, it's not Phil," Johnny said hotly. "That's why I told you not to tell anyone what the girl said. Now folks are all worked up, and they're convinced Phil did it. If they hang him, the real killer will probably go free."

The judge shook his head. "I don't see how you can be so sure Phil didn't do it. If he's tried, the girl's testimony will hang him."

"He should never be tried," Johnny shot back. "In the first place, Annie told me it was dark and the killer had a pillowcase over his head. Her testimony would be questioned by any defense lawyer, wouldn't it? She claims she recognized him by his voice and build. I don't think the prosecutor could make that stick."

Herald scratched his head and nodded. "He'd have trouble, all right."

"And another thing," Johnny went on. "Doc told me that Mrs. Engel struggled with the killer and scratched the side of his face. Well, I've seen Phil and he has no scratches on his face."

The four men stared at Johnny, all of them shocked; then Schuman said, "Of course I haven't seen him, so I don't know about that. I guess I'd just figured his face would be scratched all to hell. From the way Mrs. Engel's fingernails looked, she must have given the killer a good one."

"But why would the girl accuse Phil?" Ed Allen asked. "It doesn't seem reasonable that a sane human being would do a thing like that."

"I can tell you, though I'm not sure you'll believe me," Johnny said. "Since I work for Hawk, we've been together quite a bit and I've had several meals in his home. I guess I know Phil as well as anyone. That's the real reason I'm sure he didn't do it. I'd believe one of you men was guilty before I'd believe it was Phil, or that I'd gone out of my head long enough to do it and not remember what I'd done."

"You're on very shaky ground, Johnny," the judge said. "In my time I've known some good men to commit horrible crimes. I mean, men I knew very well personally and considered among the Lord's elect."

Johnny shrugged. "Maybe so. Anyhow, Phil's had his

share of trouble just being Hawk's kid brother. He doesn't have any interest in girls, maybe because he hasn't ever been able to make friends among the boys. I expect that is because he's Hawk's brother. Anyhow, Annie has lived beside him for years. She's in love with him, crazy in love, but he would never have anything to do with her. I think she's getting even with him. I think the truth is, she doesn't have the slightest notion who did it."

"That doesn't make any sense to me," Doc Schuman objected. "If she's in love with Phil, she sure wouldn't try to destroy him."

"It makes a lot of sense, Doc," Ed Allen said. "I've seen this kind of thing happen time after time. Love and hate are as close as that." He held up two fingers pressed tightly together. "If love is rejected, it can turn into hate."

Judge Herald nodded thoughtfully. "I think so, Doc. Maybe she said that this morning when she was upset and more or less hysterical, but after she calms down, or at least if Philip was being tried, she wouldn't swear it was him."

"That's what I think," Johnny said. "I've held off arresting him because it's more or less of a disgrace to go to jail. Besides, I know what Hawk will do when he gets back. I've sent for him, but he's so bullheaded, I don't look for him to come any sooner than he said he would."

"I expect you're right," Herald said. "This is part of the trouble. Hawk's bullheaded, all right, but he's a lot of other things that are worse. He's driven the lawless element of this camp to the place where they're ready to murder him."

The preacher leaned back in his chair and laced his fingers behind his head. He said, "Gentlemen, this conversation has clarified some points that have bothered me. I will admit, Johnny, that I have mentally and even verbally accused you of neglect of duty. I now apologize, but our basic problem, and I say ours because I consider it a problem which belongs to every decent person in Pulpit Rock, is how to save Philip's life."

"You mean you're that sure there will be an attempt to lynch him?" Royal asked.

"I do," Allen said.

Johnny nodded. "So do I. I'm glad to hear you say

73

what you did about this problem belonging to every decent person in town. I figured I was alone. I found out one thing for certain this morning. Vince Trollinger will not give any help."

"No, he sure won't," Royal said, "unless he can figure out something good for him out of it." He cleared his throat nervously, then he added, "I'm scared. I don't like to buck Charlie Roundtree and his bunch, and they're the ones who are after Hawk. They'll be the ones carrying the rope to hang Philip. Oh, I guess there'll be some miners and a few honest businessmen in the crowd, but it'll be the tough element that's going to force this. They'll be drunk and mean, and blood is going to be shed before this is over."

Johnny grinned as he rolled another cigarette. He'd had very little respect for the banker, considering him weak-kneed and possessing a backbone of jelly, but now he saw a different expression on Royal's face, a grimness, a determination that he had never seen there before.

"I'm riding out of this camp as soon as Hawk shows up," Johnny said. "Jan and I are getting married, and we're going back home. One reason is that the gamblers and the pimps and the whores run the town. The second reason is that men like you and the miners and Vince Trollinger have let them do it. Dave, you keep on talking, because you kind o' started out like you were going to say what I've been wanting to hear for a long time."

"I'll say it even if I am scared," Royal said. "I guess I'm not so scared that I'll keep my mouth shut. You're dead right about us letting the toughs run the camp, and all four of us know it. That's the real reason we're here. We'll help you, Johnny, but we wouldn't, or maybe couldn't, help Hawk Fremont."

Herald nodded. "That's right. What do you want us to do?"

"I suppose I'll have to bring Phil in," Johnny said reluctantly. "He'd better be disgraced than lynched. I don't think I can hold a mob off by myself, and I figure we'll have a lynch mob show up about dark. That's when I'll need help."

"We'll be here," Allen said. "Have you got enough guns?"

"Plenty of guns and ammunition," Johnny said. "I

74

suggest we break it into shifts. Three at a time should be enough. Judge, you and Doc take it until midnight, and then Dave and the parson take it till dawn. That agreeable?"

They all nodded, then Judge Herald said, "Go get the boy. We'll wait till you fetch him. I'd like to talk to him."

Johnny rose and left the jail. He turned toward the Fremont house, filled for the first time that day with the warm and pleasant feeling that he was not alone, that he would have help when he needed it.

He reached the corner just as Philip rode into the street from the alley back of his house. The instant he saw Johnny, he dug steel into his horse's flanks and rocketed by Johnny in a cloud of street dust, ignoring Johnny's shout, "Hold up, Phil."

One thought burned through Johnny's mind: *To most of the people of Pulpit Rock the boy's flight would be a confession of murder and robbery and rape.*

CHAPTER 14

Johnny started to run after Phil's horse, then stopped when he realized how stupid it was. He considered firing a shot over the boy's head and decided against it. Phil would know he'd never shoot to hit him.

The only thing Johnny could do was to saddle his horse and go after Phil, but it would be a tough job catching him with the head start he had. Johnny started to run again, intending to turn at the corner toward the livery stable. He knew now with the wisdom of hindsight that he should have locked Phil up this morning, but the last thing he expected was for the boy to run.

Johnny heard yelling from the business block. He didn't think it meant anything. Probably there were still men standing around talking on the street and they'd seen Phil just about the time he'd made the turn at the corner. Then, with Phil in the middle of the block, in front of the courthouse, someone fired a shot. The horse reared and went down, sending Phil off his back in a pinwheeling fall. He lay there, knocked cold.

The crowd yelled, a spine-chilling, blood-lusting yell that was unlike any sound Johnny had ever heard. The men started pounding along the street toward Phil's motionless body, but Johnny was closer and faster. By cutting across the corner of the courthouse yard, he reached Phil twenty feet or more ahead of the leaders of the crowd.

Johnny faced the men, gun in his hand. He stood astride Phil's motionless body, not knowing whether the boy was alive or not. "Hold it," he ordered. "Stand where you are."

He saw the Lawler boys in the crowd, Saul Moffat, and Jake Norton, the restaurant man. Farther back he saw Charlie Roundtree and Vince Trollinger. He knew some of the others, but most of them were miners he had seen in the saloons or on the street, men whose faces were familiar but whose names were not known to him.

The crowd ground to a halt, someone in the back yelling for him to get away from Phil and they'd take care of him. He didn't move, and for a moment none of them had the courage to charge and run the risk of getting the first bullet.

Tim Muldoon, Antoinette's bouncer, bulled his way to the front, shouting, "No tin-star deputy is gonna stop us, boys. We're gonna hang that raping kid." He lunged at Johnny, who side-stepped and brought his gun barrel chopping down on top of the big man's head. Muldoon sprawled full length in the dust, his head inches away from Phil's feet.

"Go on back to where you were," Johnny said. "I'm locking the boy up. If anybody tries that again, he'll get a dose of lead in his brisket."

"You busted his head, Jones," Saul Moffat said. "He's my friend. I'm gonna get you for this."

"You've sure got poor judgment in picking friends," Johnny snapped. "Go on now. I'm done talking."

Doc Schuman was there then, kneeling beside Phil and feeling for his pulse. Allen, Herald, and Royal waited at the edge of the street. Johnny stepped away from Phil so he wouldn't be in the doctor's way.

"We're taking Tim," Moffat said.

"Not yet," Johnny said. "You're not getting that close."

Schuman motioned to Dave Royal to help him with Phil. Together they lifted the boy and carried him to the jail. The crowd had backed away, and now as Johnny moved off the street toward the courthouse, the men surged forward.

Johnny saw the stableman, Jasper Hicks, and called, "Jasper, shoot the horse if it's necessary. In any case, get him off the street."

"I'll take care of it," Hicks said.

Moffat stood over Muldoon, his hands fisted at his sides. His pale-blue eyes, set close together astride a thin nose, were stone hard as he glared at Johnny. He said, "Jones, if you've killed Tim, I'm going to kill you. That's a promise."

Johnny holstered his gun. "Let's say he just died, Moffat. Never put off until tomorrow what you can do today. I hate waiting."

Saul Moffat carried a Colt in his holster, and Johnny knew he had at least one derringer in his pocket. He had a reputation as a killer, and Johnny had heard he'd shot three men over quarrels that had arisen out of poker games, but now, facing Johnny, he lacked the courage to finish what he had started.

"I'll wait," he said. "You can sweat it out, knowing what's coming."

"I told you I hated waiting. Maybe I'll come after you."

Moffat pretended not to hear as he and Jake Norton picked Muldoon up and carried him toward the Belle Union. Johnny raised his voice above the rumble of the crowd. "I'm keeping Phil in jail. If any of you try to take him, I'll kill you."

He wasn't sure they heard or paid any attention if they did hear. The crowd was breaking into groups and moving back into the business block. Moffat and Norton disappeared from Johnny's view, still carrying the unconscious Muldoon.

There would probably be no more trouble today, Johnny thought as he angled across the courthouse yard to the jail, but it would come later, probably sometime during the night. Saul Moffat would stir it up if no one else did.

When he reached the jail, he found Doc Schuman standing beside the cot where they had laid Phil. The other three men were lined up against the wall behind the doctor. Johnny glanced at Phil, who was motionless, his eyes closed, his face very pale, then turned to Schuman.

"Well, Doc?" Johnny asked.

"I dunno," Schuman said. "I just dunno. He had a hell of a hard fall. Looks like he landed on his head and shoulders. He doesn't have any broken bones that I can find, but he's hurt. I'll stay here until he comes out of it. That may be a long time. I don't know that I can do anything for him, but I want to be here. You never know about an injury like this. He may be paralyzed."

"I'll go see Annie," Johnny said. "She ought to be awake by now, hadn't she?"

Schuman nodded. "Go ahead." He had been staring at Philip, but now he turned his gaze to Johnny's face. "Why did he do a stupid trick like this? It's just going to make folks more certain than ever that he did it. If he'd got out of town, you'd have had to go after him."

"I sure would," Johnny said. "I don't know why he did it. I would have jailed him this morning if I'd thought he'd try to run, but he's been alone all day, so maybe he just couldn't stand it any longer. Actually he's been alone all his life. It's the price he's had to pay for being Hawk's brother."

"We could have helped if we'd known," Ed Allen said. "The feeling of being alone is one of the most deadly known to man or boy. A girl or woman, too, I guess."

"I won't be gone long," Johnny said. "Why don't you fellows go home and sleep a little if you can. Judge, you and Doc will be here at six?"

"We'll be here," Herald said.

Johnny left then, glancing toward the business block. He did not see anyone. It would be a long, hard night, he thought. They would come as surely as the sun would go down this evening and rise again in the morning.

He remembered the story of the Dutch boy holding back the flood by keeping his finger in the hole in the dike. Now he wasn't sure that all five of them could hold the flood back.

CHAPTER 15

When Vince Trollinger stopped at the Belle Union in the morning, he found the saloon empty except for the swamper, so he went on to the livery stable, ordered Jasper Hicks to harness his driving mare and hook her up to his buggy, and then drove down the canyon.

Usually he did not take a long drive, but he did this morning. For one thing, he was angry at the deputy for thinking that he'd help keep the peace, which was what Jones was paid to do, and because he'd had the effrontery to call him "Trollinger," as if they were equals. When he had been Jones's age, he'd had plenty of respect for older men who were important in his community, and Trollinger expected the same respect from all the young pups in Pulpit Rock.

The meeting with Jones rankled more than it should. He realized that as he wheeled along the side of the red cliff that formed the north wall of the canyon. The truth was that he would not have been nearly so irritated if he had not been in a highly nervous state anyhow.

Mrs. Engel's murder and robbery were what had upset him, he told himself. The raping of the girl, too. Messy crimes, crimes against decent women that offended any man who had a spark of decency in him. But later he admitted to himself that what really bothered him was his hesitancy—stupidity it seemed to him now—about accepting the offer for his property.

At first he just couldn't make up his mind, but now that he had decided to sell, he wanted the deal to go through so much that the thought of anything going wrong made him sick.

Now he could do nothing except wait until morning and then send the wire of acceptance, hoping it would be delivered in time. He knew very well that the deal swung on that very point, because there had been a good many occasions in the past when telegrams sent from Pulpit Rock had not been delivered in Denver for several hours.

He drove farther than he had intended. When he noticed how far he had come, he swung around and started back, but it was afternoon when he reached Pulpit Rock and turned the mare over to Jasper Hicks in the livery stable. He knew that dinner would be ready and Maggie would be angry because he wasn't back in time to eat it, but he hadn't had a drink today. He decided to stop in the Belle Union long enough to have just one before he went home.

The Belle Union was crowded. This surprised him. Usually Sunday was a slack day because most of the customers had had a long, rough Saturday night. He ordered his drink and stood looking at the crowd for a time before he picked up the glass and drank. He set the glass down, puzzled by what was happening.

A number of men had been in the street, but he hadn't paid any attention to them. Now he noticed that the men in the saloon were both miners and townsmen. Some of them were gamblers like Saul Moffat and others were pimps and bouncers from across the creek, like Tim Muldoon, but most of them were not of that class. Ted Riley from Trollinger's office and Jake Norton, the restaurant man, were typical—men who usually were with their families on a Sunday afternoon.

There was something else he couldn't quite put his finger on, a low, buzzing conversation that wasn't natural. No laughter, no jokes, no poker game in progress, not even much drinking going on. He heard scraps of ugly talk: "We'll hang that bastard," and "Jones oughtta be strung up for protecting the kid," and "No woman is safe as long as he's out of jail."

Charlie Roundtree joined him, smiling slightly as he said, "You going to join the mob?"

"What mob?"

Roundtree made a broad, all-inclusive gesture. "The lynch mob. I'll give these boys about another hour, and they'll go busting out of here, and somebody will find a rope. They'll go to the Fremont house, and they'll drag young Fremont out, and they'll string him up to the first cottonwood they can find."

Trollinger knew then. Lynch fever was an epidemic that had seized almost every man in the saloon. He looked at Ted Riley, whom he had known intimately for more than five years. Now he realized he had never seen the man, not the Ted Riley who was standing on the other side of the room talking to several miners. Trollinger knew he was watching a lynch mob being born, and suddenly he remembered what Johnny Jones had said about what could happen.

"Ain't you going to stop it?" Trollinger asked.

Roundtree smiled again, a bland smile that came close to saying Vince Trollinger was an idiot. "I'm afraid not, Vince. As you can see, I'm not having any part in forming it, but I sure as hell won't stop it."

Trollinger was remembering some other things now, among them the stipulation that the offer for his property depended on the removal of Hawk Fremont. Roundtree had agreed to take care of this. He asked, "What about the sheriff?"

"We're waiting," Roundtree said. "The business this morning changed our plans. There's no hurry about rubbing Fremont out. If his brother is strung up, I've got a hunch we won't have to do the chore. Hawk will get back to town foaming at the mouth. The odds are he'll rub himself out. He can't kill off a whole mining camp because his brother was lynched, and if I know Hawk, that's what he'll try to do."

"That will be too late for me," Trollinger said hoarsely. "You promised—"

"Hold on now," Roundtree interrupted. "I'll keep the promises I make, but I didn't say when. If the Denver boys still want to buy, they'll wait another day or two."

"You don't know that they will. You promised—"

"Damn it, Vince, tuck your shirttail back in. I know what they'll do. Who do you think put this little deal together? Who entertained the Denver crowd when it was here? Me, Charlie Roundtree. A whole lot can be done with this camp when you and Hawk Fremont are gone. I'll tell you a few things we'll do. We'll sell stock in the mine to the public. We'll see that nobody gets into position to rake off ten per cent the way Hawk Fremont has been doing. We'll have a few rigged wheels and similar gadgets that Fremont won't stand for."

Trollinger forgot to breathe for a time. He whispered, "You? You were in this from the first?"

"That's right. Little old Charlie Roundtree. I've watched you operate for years, Vince. In some ways you're as crooked as that kid of yours. In other ways you're so honest you make me sick. No, you don't have to worry about the deal going sour. We want it, all right, but you'll have to wait until we see how this works out."

Trollinger was sick, so sick that for a little while he thought he was going to lose his drink right there. He swallowed and moistened his dry lips. He heard Roundtree laugh. He hated the saloon man, hated him worse than he had ever hated anyone in his life.

"Come on now, Vince," Roundtree said. "We'll throw the Fremont kid to the mob, and then we'll wait. We'll watch what happens. Just remember, you 'n' me had nothing to do with it."

"You don't think the kid done it?" Trollinger whispered.

Roundtree shrugged. "I don't know and I don't care. We know that the thief got four hundred dollars, so we'll see to it that four hundred dollars is found in his room. We know Doc Schuman says the killer's face was scratched, so we'll fix the kid's face with some scratches. I don't figure that Hawk can blame us—" A yell rose from the street and sent men charging out of the saloon. "Oh hell," Roundtree muttered. "What's happened now?"

He ran out of the saloon, with Trollinger a step behind. He felt as if he had been slugged on the head, slugged so hard he couldn't think straight. Charlie Roundtree had insulted him to his face, and he had done nothing. He knew he wouldn't. All he wanted was to get out of Pulpit Rock and go somewhere else and start over.

He heard a shot and saw Phil Fremont thrown from his horse; he saw the crowd—with Saul Moffat leading it—charge down the street to where young Fremont lay; and he saw Johnny Jones standing over the boy's motionless figure, a gun in his hand. The cowboy deputy stood up to Moffat, he cooled Tim Muldoon, and he saw to it that Doc Schuman and Dave Royal carried Phil Fremont to the jail.

All of this flashed before Vince Trollinger's eyes. He was a spectator but not a participant, watching one scene after another of an incredible drama which could not be taking place in his mining camp. Then he realized that it was no longer his camp. Somehow he had let Charlie Roundtree steal it right out from under his nose.

He found himself moving back with the crowd. Roundtree was beside him. He heard the saloon man say, "I always prided myself in being a good judge of men, but I missed on that damned Jones. I figured he'd be easy to handle when Hawk was out of town, but it turns out he's as tough as Hawk and a hell of a lot smarter. He might even be honest." Roundtree laid a hand on Trollinger's shoulder. "Come in and I'll buy you another drink."

"No, I'm late for dinner," Trollinger said. "I've got to go home."

He plowed his way through the crowd and walked home as fast as he could. How had he fallen into the hands of a man like Charlie Roundtree, who had never opposed him on anything? Charlie Roundtree, who had always been a smiling, pleasant man, never demanding anything, so mild he had seemed almost timid at times.

Well, he'd been wrong. Charlie Roundtree was none of those things. He, Vince Trollinger, had seen him through his own eyes. Somehow he had made up his own image. The truth was that he had been stupid. Roundtree and Moffat and even Hawk Fremont had done a lot of crooked things he had never suspected.

All right, he'd take Roundtree's money from whoever was putting it up. He didn't care. He'd get out of town and to hell with it. He was a mining man. He should have known all the time that he could never trust a gambler or a pimp or a scheming bastard like Charlie Roundtree.

The instant he entered the house, Maggie called, "Dinner's been ready for an hour. Now it's all dried out."

"I won't complain," Trollinger said. "Is Clay still home?"

"I think he's in his room," Maggie answered. "He went

83

right up there after you left, and he ain't come down as far as I know."

"He must be sick," Trollinger said. "I'll see if he wants to come down and eat with me."

He climbed the stairs hoping that Clay would say the wrong thing. He'd beat the boy to a bloody pulp. It was bad enough to be fooled by Roundtree. His own son was no better. "As crooked as your own kid," Roundtree had said.

He opened the door into Clay's room. The boy was asleep. Trollinger crossed to him and stopped, staring at the side of his face. He saw the long, raw slashes, and when he backed away and looked at the bureau, he saw the pile of greenbacks that had been tossed carelessly on the marble top—four hundred dollars in twenty-dollar bills—and then the truth hit Trollinger in the face.

Turning, he staggered out of the room and down the stairs.

CHAPTER 16

When Johnny reached the Engel house, he discovered that a saddle horse was tied to the hitch rack in front. He wondered about it as he walked up the path to the front door, then remembered that Mrs. Engel's brother was coming today to get the money she had taken out of the bank for him. The horse probably belonged to him.

The front door opened as Johnny stepped up on the porch. A fat man came out, took one look at Johnny's star, and said in a hostile voice, "I guess you're the deputy who's too stupid or stubborn to arrest the kid who done this thing."

"I'm the deputy," Johnny said, thinking it was easy to dislike this man. "I suppose you're Mrs. Engel's brother she was going to loan the money to."

"That's right," the fat man said. "Lud Montgomery's the name. I've got to go back to Ouray 'cause I work tomorrow. Mrs. Bolger, she says she'll look after Annie and will arrange for the funeral. I'll be back for that. Now

I'll tell you something, mister. If the kid ain't been arrested by the time I get here, I'll go after him myself."

Johnny knew there was no use arguing with a man like this, no use telling him that Annie had lied about Phil. If he stayed and tried to talk to the stranger, his temper, already close to the breaking point, would snap and he'd probably end up beating the fat man half to death. So he stepped around Montgomery and went into the house.

Mrs. Bolger sat in a rocking chair near an open window in the front room. She said, "He ain't a very nice man, Mr. Jones. I've knowed him for several years. He's the youngest one in the family, and I guess he was spoiled rotten when he was little. Anyhow, Mrs. Engel has given him money off and on, and he's sure been happy to sponge off her."

Johnny watched from a window until Montgomery mounted and rode off; then he said, "I suppose he was more concerned about having the money stolen than his sister being murdered."

"That's exactly the way he talked," Mrs. Bolger said grimly. "I never have liked him, and I like him even less now. He didn't talk to Annie very nice, so I told him to leave. He wouldn't until I got me a rolling pin out of the kitchen, and I said I'd bust his head if he didn't. He left when I said that, all right."

"Annie's awake then?"

Mrs. Bolger nodded. "I fixed her some coffee, and she feels purty good now."

"I'm going to talk to her," Johnny said. "She can save Phil's life if she'll do it. See if you can rustle some paper and ink and a pen. I want a statement from her if she'll give it to me."

Mrs. Bolger rose and crossed the room to a desk. "It's all right here, Mr. Jones. Mrs. Engel had a big family, and she wrote lots of letters. I'll lay it out. When you're ready for it, just holler, and I'll fetch it in."

Johnny went into the girl's bedroom, pulled up a chair, and sat down beside the bed. A damp towel lay across her forehead and her eyes were red from crying. Now she looked at Johnny and suddenly the tears began to flow again.

"Now wait a minute, Annie," Johnny said softly. "I

don't want to make you start crying. I just wanted to talk about Phil."

"I knew that was what you wanted," Annie whispered. "I tell you he did it, so there's no use of you nagging me about it. He did it, I tell you. He did it."

She turned her face to stare at the wall. She dabbed at her eyes, but she wasn't crying. She had shed all the tears that she could, he thought. He waited for a time, sitting motionless as he watched her. Then he said, "Annie, do you hate Phil so much that you want to see him hang?"

Slowly she turned her head so she could see him. She said, "Hate him? Mr. Jones, I love him. I've loved him for a long time. I've lived beside him for two years and I've told him how I felt and I've asked him to take me to parties and I've tried to walk to school with him, but he wouldn't have anything to do with me."

She started to cry again. He waited silently until she stopped. For a minute or more she whimpered like a small child; then, when that too stopped, he asked, "Do you want to hang him, Annie?"

She swallowed, and suddenly her body shook with great racking sobs. Johnny didn't say a word. Mrs. Bolger came into the room and stood beside the bed, looking down at Annie. "Mr. Jones, I don't think she's able—"

"I'm all right, Mrs. Bolger," the girl said. "I just get the weepies, but I'm all right." She swallowed and moistened her dry lips with the tip of her tongue. "Do you know what it is to love someone so much you just live for a word or . . . a smile? Just to know that he knows you're alive? Do you know how much you ache way down inside when you go for days and weeks and you don't get either a word or a smile?"

"I know he's hurt you very much and I'm sorry," Johnny said, "but that doesn't change his innocence. You see, I know he didn't do it, and I know you're lying about being sure it was him. Your mother fought with the murderer and she scratched him on the cheek. Pretty bad, the doctor says, judging from the skin and blood that were under her fingernails.

"Well, Annie, the murderer can't wash those scratches off his face. They'll be there for several days until they heal. When I find a man with scratches like that, I'll work on him until I get the truth out of him. This is how I know it's not Phil. He doesn't have a mark on his face."

Annie stared at him, blinking, her lips parted. He hurried on, "If you love him, I want you to think how you'll feel if you are the cause of his death. After you said it was Phil this morning, Doctor Schuman told other people it was him, and now everybody in town thinks he did it. They'll probably try to lynch him. With Hawk gone, I'm not sure I can stop them."

She still didn't say anything, and he couldn't tell whether she understood what he had told her. He went on, "Phil's been alone all day in the house. He couldn't stand it any longer, so he saddled his horse and tried to leave town, but somebody shot his horse, and he was hurt when the horse threw him. If I hadn't been there, the mob would have killed him. He's in jail now, and I'll do all I can to protect him, but it would help if you sign a paper saying you lied this morning and it wasn't Phil." He paused, and then he said, "Annie, if you will do that, Phil will know you saved his life."

"Maybe he'll give me a smile if I do," she said wistfully. "All right, I'll sign a paper if it will help. You tell him I'm sorry I caused him so much trouble."

Johnny gestured toward Mrs. Bolger. She left the room and returned with pen and ink and a tablet. Johnny said, "I'll write it and you can sign it, but you'll have to tell me what to write."

She reached for the tablet. "Let me write it," she said. "You hold the bottle of ink."

"All right," he said, and gave her the pen and pulled the cork from the ink bottle.

She dipped the pen into the ink and began to write; then she signed her name and handed the tablet back to Johnny. He read aloud:

> I lied this morning when I said Phil killed my mother and robbed us. I don't know who it was because he had a pillowcase over his head, but he was a big man and not slender like Phil. I did not hear his voice. I swear before God this is true.

> ANNIE ENGEL

"That's fine, Annie," Johnny said. "I'll tell Phil first thing when I get back to the jail."

"Tell him to come and see me as soon as he can," she said.

Johnny rose. "You stay there and rest. Would you like for the doctor to see you this afternoon?"

"No, I'll be all right," she said.

Mrs. Bolger followed Johnny out of the room. She said in a low tone, "There's something fishy about this, Mr. Jones. If the man who done the killing had a pillowcase over his head, how did he get his face scratched?"

Johnny whistled softly. "Now that's an interesting question. I never thought of it." He folded the sheet of paper and slipped it into his pocket. "I don't suppose we'll ever know for sure because Mrs. Engel's dead and the killer ain't likely to tell us. All we know is that it did happen. Doc wouldn't lie about it, and I don't see any reason for Annie to lie about his face being covered. Besides, I found a wadded-up pillowcase in the alley this morning that had eyeholes cut in it."

"Mrs. Engel could have jerked the pillowcase off his head before he hit her," Mrs. Bolger suggested. "Maybe that's why he killed her. He knew she could have identified him."

"Sounds reasonable," Johnny agreed. "Or he might have been hunting for the money and took it off because it bothered him. Maybe she woke up and saw him. Like you just said, he knew she could have identified him, so he killed her. Well, I've got to get back. You can stay here with Annie. I'm going to keep Johnny in jail. I don't even know how bad he's hurt."

"I think I'd better stay," Mrs. Bolger said. "Annie can't be left alone."

As Johnny stepped outside, he glanced at the sun, which was far down in the west. It would be time for supper soon, and he didn't know whether Jake Norton would bring him and Phil a meal or not, but Johnny doubted that he would. Johnny didn't have time to go to his cabin and fix anything. He couldn't leave Phil alone in the jail that long.

When he got back, he found that the four men were still there. He said, "I thought you'd all be gone but Doc."

"We got a little uneasy after you left," the judge said. "There's always a point of explosion in a situation like this, and we might be close to it. Mobs are funny. They're as unpredictable as April weather. You never know what they're going to do or when they'll do it, so we thought we'd better stay till you got back anyway."

"Oh, I don't think we'll see 'em till after it's dark," Johnny said. "I told you to go home and get some sleep."

"Oh, you don't think they'll come till dark, do you?" Dave Royal asked from the doorway. "Well, maybe you'd better take a look."

Johnny wheeled to the door. A crowd of men had just spilled around the corner and was headed straight toward the jail. Saul Moffat was leading them, a rope in his hands.

CHAPTER 17

For a moment Johnny stood paralyzed, watching the crowd pour around the corner into the street, cross it, and come on to the courthouse yard. He wondered if there was any end to the line. They kept coming, one hundred of them or more, five or six abreast, moving slowly with the determination of a restless current that would overrun anything in its path.

Suddenly Johnny realized he had only seconds to prepare for them. He had been completely wrong in thinking that a lynch mob would not make a move in daylight, that the men in it would be afraid to be seen and identified. He had not talked to the four men with him about what to do, but now he wheeled to the gunrack, thankful that they were still here.

"Doc," he called.

He handed Winchesters to Royal, Allen, and Judge Herald; then Schuman came out of the side room and took the rifle that Johnny pressed into his hands, a questioning expression on his face that was not answered until Johnny grabbed a double-barreled shotgun and ran to the door.

"Dave and Ed, take that window." He pointed to the one on the left side of the door. "The judge and Doc take the other one. Poke the barrels of your rifles out so they can see 'em, but don't shoot unless I do."

He stepped through the door, one hammer of the shotgun eared back. The leaders of the mob were not more than thirty or forty feet away when Johnny said, "Stop. Right there. This shotgun is loaded with buckshot, and it makes one hell of a hole in a man. Moffat, if you keep coming, you'll get the first load."

The gambler stopped, motioning for the others to halt. They did stop just as they had on the street an hour or so before, but there was a difference. That had been a spontaneous explosion of action, triggered by Phil's appearance in the street and the shot that had knocked the boy's horse down.

Now Johnny had the feeling, as he looked at the men who had fanned out to form a semicircle in front of the jail, that there was a terrible blood-lusting fever in them that demanded blood before it would abate.

"We've come for the Fremont kid," Moffat said, his tone ominous. "If you stand there in our way, we'll hang you, too. Now put that scattergun down and get out of the doorway."

"No, Moffat," Johnny said. "The boy is in jail. I thought that was what you wanted."

"We want more than that," Moffat said. "We've been talking and we decided it was time we did something more than talk. There are decent women in this camp. We aim to make sure they are protected and not be afraid some man or boy is going to break into their house and attack them."

"If Phil is the man you want," Johnny said, "the women are safe. I told you he's in jail."

"Oh hell," Moffat said in disgust. "He'll go free the minute Hawk Fremont gets back to town. We're going to see justice is done so he can't turn the kid loose."

"Phil ain't the man you want," Johnny said. "I have a statement signed by Annie Engel saying she lied when she accused Phil of the murder of her mother. She don't know who did it."

"Now you're lying," Moffat said, "but if you do have

such a statement, the girl gave it under duress. You probably beat her till she signed it."

"You're a liar," Johnny said hotly. "Get out of here. All of you."

"We'll give you ten seconds to clear the doorway," Moffat said, "and save your life. If you're not out of the doorway, we're coming in."

"Don't start counting those ten seconds yet," Johnny said. "There are four men in the jail with rifles. You look up at the windows and you'll see the rifle barrels. I've got two loads in this scattergun. Now there's enough of you to overrun the jail and take us, but while you're doing it, we'll kill two men apiece. If the ten who are in front figure this is worth dying for, come ahead."

The seconds ticked away, a tense silence falling on the mob. Tim Muldoon, with a bandage around his head, was in the front row. So were the Lawler boys. Behind them Johnny saw Ted Riley and Jake Norton. There were others he knew. His gaze swept the sea of faces only once and then fixed on Moffat, the shotgun pointing at the gambler's belly.

Johnny had no notion of passing time, though he was certain that more than the ten seconds Moffat had given him had passed. No one seemed to breathe; no one said a word; and even with the determination that was in these men, the ones in front knew that Johnny was right. They would be the first to die.

Johnny felt the pulse pound in his forehead; his lips were dry; but he knew that the one thing he must not do was to take his gaze off Saul Moffat. If he could break the gambler, the crisis would be over. The rest would cave in and retreat.

The trouble was that Saul Moffat was trapped. He had no more desire to die than the other men in front, but he was the leader. If he broke after committing himself and coming this far, he'd have to leave Pulpit Rock, a fact that certainly was known to him.

The silent waiting seemed endless, then it broke in a way that was totally unexpected by Johnny. One of the rifles cracked behind him, and a man far out on the edge of the crowd yelled in pain.

For an instant the men turned to see who had yelled, and Johnny took advantage of that shift of attention. He

91

leaped forward, grabbed Moffat by a shoulder, and spun him around, the muzzle of the shotgun rammed between his shoulder blades.

"Go on," he ordered. "The whole kit and caboodle of you. I've had enough of this."

"That's right." Judge Herald stood in the doorway behind Johnny, his cocked rifle covering Tim Muldoon. "I'm surprised at some of you letting yourselves be led around this way by a gambler like Moffat and a tough from a brothel, like Muldoon. Jake, I thought you were a law-abiding man. Ted, I hope Vince Trollinger fires you for this. Jasper, I've had you on juries and I've heard you on the witness stand, and by God, I thought you were a man."

The grim determination leaked out of them like air escaping through a hole in a balloon. The judge was the most respected man in Pulpit Rock, and his harsh words had an immediate effect. Several men simply turned and walked away. Jake Norton and Jasper Hicks were the first to move. Ted Riley followed, then the miners began edging away, and a moment later only the toughs were still there.

"Come on, Saul," Muldoon said. "I'll get that bastard some other time for caving my head in."

Still Moffat hesitated, the back of his neck turning red. Then he cursed and strode away, not looking back. Five minutes later the mob had disappeared. Only the wounded man remained. His name was Percy Lamar, a pimp from Antoinette's place, a small, elegantly dressed man who held his bullet-shattered right arm with his left. He was moaning as he staggered toward the jail, blood dripping from his injured arm.

"Is Doc in there?" Lamar cried shrilly. "I've got to have this arm fixed."

"You aimed to shoot Johnny, didn't you?" the judge asked. "You figured that if he was down, the mob would start moving again. They might have done it, too." He glanced at Johnny, who had backed up to lean against the front wall of the jail. "I saw him pull his gun. Nobody else was moving, so I decided I'd better let him have it in spite of your orders not to shoot."

"Thanks," Johnny said. "I'd probably be dead if you hadn't shot him."

Doc Schuman stood in the doorway, glaring at the moaning Lamar. "Come in here," Schuman said. "You're the poorest excuse for a man there is in this whole camp, and your stinking life isn't worth saving, but I've got to try anyway."

Schuman stepped aside and Lamar stumbled into the jail. Johnny looked at the judge and tried to grin, but his mouth seemed frozen. He wiped a hand across his sweaty face and suddenly realized he was trembling.

The judge smiled, his bony old face showing no concern whatever. "It was kind of touch and go there for a minute or two, wasn't it?"

"Yeah, it sure was," Johnny muttered. "I was scared, Judge. I wasn't scared a while ago in the street when Phil's horse threw him, but it was different just now. Seemed like all that bunch was hell bent to do what they set out to do."

"That's right," the judge agreed. "If Lamar hadn't made his move, I don't know how long it would have gone on." He scratched the tip of his nose, frowning; then he added, "It did me good to be here with a thirty-thirty in my hands again, Johnny. It's a strange thing, but I've seen it happen more than once. Five men with guts can hold off better than a hundred."

"They'll be back," Johnny said. "I've been wrong more'n once today. I was dead sure they wouldn't make a move until dark, but I know damn well I'm not wrong on this. They'll be back."

Herald nodded. "I'm sure they will, but it won't be the whole bunch. A lot of them are going to be hard to pull into another mob. Chances are, most of them are glad it turned out this way." His face turned somber. "Lynching a man is something you never forget, and you never forgive yourself for being a part of it."

The old man was speaking from experience, Johnny thought, but he didn't press Herald for an explanation. He said, "I'm going in and see Phil."

When he stepped back into the sheriff's office, Johnny saw that Lamar was sitting at the desk and Schuman was working on him. Royal and Allen were watching. He went on into the side room and pulled a chair up to the side of the cot. The boy lay on his back, his eyes open.

"How do you feel?" Johnny asked.

"Like hell," Phil answered. "Why didn't you let them hang me? Hawk would rather see me dead than the way I am."

"Why do you say that?"

"I'm paralyzed," Phil said. "I can't move a muscle below my neck. You think Hawk will have any use for me when he finds out?"

Johnny rose and walked to the window and stood staring out at the weed-covered yard bathed in the late-afternoon sunlight. He couldn't sit there and look at the boy. Phil was right. Hawk Fremont had no patience with weakness of any kind.

CHAPTER 18

Johnny left the side room and walked to the desk in the sheriff's office, where Doc Schuman sat, tipped back in the swivel chair, eyes on the ceiling. Allen and Judge Herald were seated in the rawhide-bottom chairs that were set against the west wall. Royal stood in the doorway, his back against the casing.

"We think we'd all better stay here tonight," Schuman said. "Much as I hate to miss my sleep, I don't think it's safe to have just three of us here at one time. Five can throw more lead than three if it comes to that."

Herald nodded agreement. "That's right. Maybe we can get some sleep in one of the cells. We think it's important for all of us to be here. Even if we are asleep, we can wake up enough to shoot, but if we're home in bed, it'll take us fifteen minutes or more to get here after the shooting starts. That would be too late."

Allen and Royal nodded, Allen saying, "If we stay till daylight, I think you'll be safe. The men who were here this afternoon will see this proposition a lot different after they sleep on it. Besides, most of them go to work early."

"I'll be relieved to have you here all night," Johnny admitted. "It's just that I hated to have you miss sleeping. None of you will be worth a damn tomorrow."

"Oh, we'll make out," Royal said. "We'll leave as soon

as it's daylight and catch an hour or two of sleep before we have breakfast."

"I've got a funeral to preach in the afternoon," Allen said, "so I'd better be worth something."

"And I've got two babies who are scheduled to show up tomorrow," Schuman said. "Of course bankers and judges can stay in bed all day if they want to."

Herald made a jeering sound and Royal flushed angrily, but he didn't say anything. The pressure was harder on Dave Royal than any of the others, but Johnny had quit trying to guess what the man would do. He had already done more than Johnny had expected of him or even thought possible.

"Right now I'm wondering what we're going to do about supper," Johnny said. "I'd go to the Bon Ton and have Jake and his wife cook us a meal if this was an ordinary situation, and charge it to the county, but I don't much like to show up downtown. It might be enough to set things off. Besides, Jake might not do it, feeling the way he does."

"I'll go home and have my wife cook a meal," Allen said, "and I'll fetch it over after the evening service."

"Good," Johnny said. "Some sandwiches will do."

Allen rose, glanced at Herald, then said, "Judge, maybe you ought to go with me in case I've got more than I can carry. Let's take the Winchesters."

"Good idea," Herald said.

"Maybe I can get you to come to church for once."

"So that's your game," the judge said. "Well, I did miss last Easter, so I guess I owe you that much."

After they left, Dave Royal said, "The preacher's afraid. It makes me feel better just to know that somebody else is scared."

"I was scared when I was standing nose to nose with Saul Moffat a while ago," Johnny said.

The doctor laughed softly. "You didn't show it, boy. I guess that's the whole trick."

Johnny moved close to the desk. He asked in a low tone, "How about Phil?"

"I wish I knew," Schuman answered. "Right now I'm afraid he's paralyzed for life." He took his pipe out of his pocket and filled it, then added, "The longer I practice medicine, the more I realize there's something to healing

95

the human body that doesn't come under surgery or giving pills. Or any of the things we've done since the day of Hippocrates."

He nodded at Royal. "You were talking about being afraid. Ordinary fear is normal enough, but I've seen people so frightened that their bodies couldn't function. It could be that way with Phil. Maybe he'll get over his paralysis when he's not as scared as he is right now."

"I've got a hunch it depends on what Hawk says and does when he gets back," Johnny said. "I think Hawk's the one he's really afraid of."

Schuman nodded. "That's quite possible. Hawk Fremont is the kind of man who inspires fear in people. The whole camp is afraid of him. I've got a notion that's the main reason so many things have happened. Remember what Moffat said? About Phil going free the minute Hawk gets back to town? Well, you hold the lid on tight for just so long, and when enough steam has gathered, you're going to get the lid blowed off."

Johnny nodded. In effect this was what he had thought and close to what he had told Fremont and Zero Moran just before they had left town, but even in his worst nightmare he had not foreseen this situation.

He returned to the side room and sat down beside the cot again. He asked, "Think you could eat somthing? Ed Allen has gone to get some sandwiches."

"No," Phil answered. "I couldn't hold a sandwich in my hand, let alone get it up to my mouth."

Johnny was silent, thinking it would be better not to push anything now with Phil. Later, perhaps, when he was hungry enough, he would be willing to let someone else hold the sandwich. Finally he asked, "Why did you try to run away, Phil?"

"I knew you'd ask that sooner or later," the boy answered. "You'll probably think I'm lying, but I never intended to run away. I was just trying to take a ride. I was alone and I thought I was going crazy. I couldn't stay in the house any longer, and all I could think of doing was to saddle up and go for a ride."

"I told you to stay inside," Johnny reminded him.

"I know you did. That's why I wouldn't stop when you yelled at me. I figured you were going to bawl me out, and I couldn't stand it. I couldn't, Johnny. I've never been

96

able to make friends, and I guess I've never been very happy, having to depend on Hawk the way I have, but I still never dreamed that Annie would be mean enough to accuse me of a crime like that and people would believe it and want to hang me. I can't really believe it yet."

He could be telling the truth, Johnny thought. He said, "I saw Annie this afternoon. She wrote out a statement and signed it that says she lied and it wasn't you. She asked me to tell you to come and see her as soon as you could."

"Yeah," Phil said bitterly. "I'll be sure to do that."

Johnny realized there was no use in telling Phil now that Annie loved him, that she just wanted him to notice her. Maybe Phil had been right in ignoring the girl so completely. She probably would have been a pest if he had paid even a little attention to her. Living next door the way she had, it could have been a difficult situation.

He rose and went outside to stand beside Dave Royal in front of the jail. Strange, he reflected, how some people wanted to be loved and still found so little love in life from anyone. He was staring across the weed-covered yard at the courthouse, not even aware that the sun was almost down, so lost in his thoughts that he was startled when Royal said, "Jan's coming to see you."

Johnny turned and glanced along E Street. Jan was coming toward them, walking along the edge of the yard and holding her skirt high to keep it from dragging in the dirt. Johnny groaned. "This is the last place I want her to be."

He ran toward her. She stopped and waited when she saw him coming. When he reached her, she put out both hands, asking, "What's been going on? I've heard all kinds of wild stories. Are they true?"

"It's been wild, all right," he said. "You go back home and stay there. I don't know what's going to happen, but I don't want you mixed up in it."

"I'm not budging one step till you tell me about it," she said doggedly.

He told her as briefly as he could, then he said, "I've sent Rolly Poe after Hawk. If he comes back, I'm turning my star in, and you and me are getting out of here."

"And if he doesn't come back?"

"Oh, honey, you know I can't go off and leave Phil," he

said. "I'm pretty sure they'll try something before morning. By now Moffat and Muldoon and the Lawler boys figure this is personal. They probably want me as bad as they do Phil."

"They'll kill you if they can, I suppose," she said angrily. "You don't owe these people anything the way they've treated you. Me, too. I don't like them. If Mrs. Royal and Mrs. Schuman and some of the others had given me their business, I wouldn't be sewing for Antoinette, but no, I wasn't good enough for them. They went to a dressmaker in Montrose, or they got on the train and went to Denver. Let's leave now, Johnny. I want to keep you alive."

"I want to stay alive," he said, thinking he had never heard her speak as bitterly about the women of Pulpit Rock as she had just then. "I've got a lot to live for, but I can't go. You wouldn't be proud of me if I did."

She frowned, looking into his face as she thought about what he had said, then she nodded. She said reluctantly, "Isn't it funny? I'll go back to my house and sit and wait and hope that Fremont gets here soon. I know you're right. It's just that I didn't want it to be that way."

"I don't think he'll be back," Johnny said. "Not till Tuesday afternoon, which is when he said he'd be back. I think we've got about forty-eight hours to wait."

For a moment he thought she was going to cry, but she regained her composure in a few seconds. She said, "You'd better kiss me and send me about my business."

He kissed her and held her in his arms a moment, then she drew away from him and managed a smile. "I used to think that hell was made up of the smell of horses and the sound of bawling cattle and lots of dust and cactus and sagebrush, but right now all of that would be heaven."

She walked away. He stood watching until she was past the intersection of Main and E Streets, then he turned back to the jail. Allen and the judge did not return until long after dark. They brought a peach pie and a pot of coffee in addition to the sandwiches.

They ate in silence, a sliver of a moon showing above the eastern peaks, then Johnny heard a horse coming toward them from the street. He stepped outside, the shotgun in his hands. A moment later the rider reined up in front of the doorway, and in the finger of light from the lamp on the desk Johnny saw that it was Rolly Poe.

"Where's Hawk?" Johnny asked.

"I don't know where he went after I left him, and I don't give a damn," Poe said in a voice that sounded as if he was tired enough to fall out of his saddle. "You can bully me all you want to and threaten to beat hell out of me, but I'll never go after that big bastard again."

"What did he say?"

"He laughed in my face like he done before, then he got mad. He said you was a fool and you would be a worse one if you locked Phil up. He said nobody in this camp was stupid enough or had the guts to do anything to Phil, and it was up to you to keep law and order until he got back Tuesday afternoon."

Johnny took a long breath, his gaze going to the end of the business block as if he expected to see a lynch mob come around the corner again. He was dead tired. He wiped a hand across his face as he said, "Thanks, Rolly. You went to a lot of trouble for nothing, seems like, but I thought we ought to do it. Go put your horse up and go to bed."

Poe rode across the yard to E Street and turned on Main to the livery stable. Johnny returned to the jail, the eyes of the four men on him. He said, "Hawk ain't coming. I guess it's up to us."

"Well, I doubt that you really expected anything else from him," Judge Herald said. "That's typical of the arrogant way he operates."

"It's time for all good men to rise up and demand a new sheriff," Ed Allen said. "Would you take the star, Johnny?"

"I would not," he answered with more violence than he intended. "For two cents I'd get Jan's and my horses and ride out of this camp with her. Now. Right now."

"No," Doc Schuman said. "You couldn't do it, Johnny. I guess we've all learned some things about each other in the last twelve hours or so. I know I've learned a thing or two about you. Riding out of this camp before Fremont gets back is something you are no more capable of doing than I would be of failing to work on somebody who was hurt or Ed of failing to pray for someone who needed spiritual help."

"We started off wrong this morning," Royal said. "I think we're on the right track now and we can do this job."

"I think so, too," Judge Herald agreed. "Hang on till daylight, Johnny. If they don't come tonight, I don't think they're going to. The steam will be gone by then. I've watched this kind of thing more than once. What we need is time."

Johnny wheeled to the door and went outside. He stared into the darkness as he leaned against the wall. Hang on, they said. Wait, wait, wait. For what? To die?

It could end that way, he thought, for both him and Phil. But Doc Schuman was right. He couldn't ride out, not for two cents or anything else.

CHAPTER 19

Vince Trollinger went directly to his study after coming downstairs from Clay's room. Maggie called, "Ain't you ready to eat your dinner?"

"No," he yelled. "Eat it yourself."

He poured himself a stiff drink of whisky and gulped it. Maggie appeared in the doorway. "Mr. Trollinger, I worked hard fixing that dinner. It ain't clear spoiled even if it is dried out some. You ought to come—"

"You get to hell out of here," he bellowed. "Shut the door."

"Well," she said tartly, "I don't have to take that kind of treatment from you or nobody. Find yourself another housekeeper and to hell with you."

She slammed the door. He sat down at his desk and buried his face in his hands. That was where he spent the afternoon. Sometimes he would get up and pace around the room, or he would sit at his desk staring unseeingly across the room. Once a great sob shook his body and tears ran down his cheeks.

Clay Trollinger, murderer, thief, rapist. Oh, Vince Trollinger had known for a long time that his son was no account, that he drank too much and gambled too much and spent too much time in Antoinette's place, but Trollinger had told himself that these were the natural activities in which a boy indulged when he was growing up. He had footed the bill. Up until last night, anyhow.

He knew, then—knew in a sudden flash of insight that rocked his entire body—that he was to blame for what had happened. If he had given Clay what he asked for last night, the boy wouldn't have done these hideous things. Then, and this thought hit him so hard that he couldn't breathe for a moment, Philip Fremont would be lynched for a crime he had not committed. Indirectly, yes, but it was still Vince Trollinger's fault.

He couldn't let it happen. He rose with the intention of going to Johnny Jones and telling him the truth. He sat down again. He couldn't do it.

For a long time he wrestled with this problem, not knowing what to do. He had always considered himself a reasonably decent human being. Oh, he was a hard man to do business with. If anyone owed him a nickel, he collected with interest when the debt was due. He never paid his men a cent of wages he didn't have to, and he worked them as many hours as he could. Still, as far as he knew, he had never actually broken any laws. But his son had.

Now he was impaled on the horns of a dilemma. If he remained silent, Philip Fremont would be lynched for a crime he had not committed. On the other hand, he could not go to Jones and tell him that his son was the murderer and thief and rapist the law was looking for. Even if the people of Pulpit Rock knew the truth, they wouldn't lynch Clay. No one would think of laying a hand on a Trollinger. He might not even be convicted if he were tried.

Still, there would be talk and a certain amount of disgrace that Vince Trollinger couldn't face. If he knew for sure the deal for his property was going through ... Then he sat bolt upright. When the Denver men heard what had happened, they'd withdraw their offer. They had insisted they wanted a law-abiding camp; they had also insisted that Hawk Fremont be removed; and right now it looked as if neither one of the requirements would be met.

He paced the floor again. He drank too much whisky; he smoked too many cigars. Suddenly he was aware that the afternoon was gone and he had done nothing. But what was there to do? He could not concentrate; he could not make a decision.

All he knew was that he didn't give a damn whether the mob strung young Fremont up or not. Then he knew something else. No matter what Clay had done, he was his son, his flesh and blood; he was a Trollinger. He would do anything and everything he could to keep the boy from being found out.

He lighted a lamp and sat down at his desk. His mind was fuzzy. His tongue felt as if it had been burned; the inside of his mouth had gone bone dry. He put his head down on his arms and for a while lost all track of time.

Then, hours later, he sat up, his fists clenched. He knew. It had come clear. If Philip Fremont was lynched, the case would be closed. The people of Pulpit Rock would have avenged the murder of Mrs. Engel and the rape of her daughter. No one would suspect Clay. All the boy had to do was to stay in the house for a few days until his scratches healed.

If Philip hadn't been hung already, it was time the mob was getting at it. If Charlie Roundtree was still just a spectator, he'd better be doing something. Give a few more free drinks, say a few more things about women and girls not being safe in Pulpit Rock as long as Philip Fremont was alive. Roundtree could do it and still not be suspected of having any part in the lynching.

Trollinger ran out of the house, feverish in his hurry to see Roundtree and build a fire under him. Trollinger didn't know why he'd sat around all afternoon and most of the evening doing nothing. But it wasn't too late. It couldn't be.

Main Street was deserted. Most of the saloons were closed. When Trollinger reached the Belle Union and pushed the bat wings apart and stepped inside, he couldn't believe what he saw. The place was empty except for one bartender, who was cleaning up.

"Where's Charlie?" Trollinger demanded.

The bartender nodded amiably. "Good evening, Mr. Trollinger. Charlie said you'd probably be in sometime and I was to give you a drink on the house and tell you to go home."

"Oh no, I'm not going home," Trollinger said loudly. "Not till I see Charlie. Where is everybody?"

"Gone," the bartender said. "It's after ten. We always close early on Sunday night." He set a bottle and a glass on the cherry-wood bar. "Take your drink and go home and I'll lock up. We've had a busy day and I'm tired."

"I don't want your damned drink," Trollinger said angrily. "What's more, I'm not one of your barflies who can't afford to pay for his drink. I want to see Charlie."

The bartender shook his head. "I'm sorry, Mr. Trollinger. Charlie and Saul have gone upstairs and are probably in bed by now. They said not to disturb them under any circumstances."

Probably they were in bed, Trollinger thought, with a couple of women they'd brought from the other side of the creek, something which was not allowed. They would not have done it if Hawk Fremont had been in town.

"Go upstairs and get Charlie," Trollinger said. "I'm going to see him and I'm going to see him now. If you don't get him, I'll go up those stairs and I'll kick his goddamn door down."

"Mr. Trollinger, I'm afraid you're drunk," the bartender said. "I don't want any trouble with you. I know what my orders were. Please go home."

"Not till I see Charlie," Trollinger said.

He started along the bar toward the stairs that led to the balcony. "Hold it, Mr. Trollinger," the bartender said. "Hold it right there."

Trollinger reached the foot of the stairs. He stopped and took a long breath. The fool had picked up a sawed-off shotgun, had eared the hammer back, and was pointing the gun at him.

"All right, Vince," Roundtree called from the balcony. "I'll come down if it's that important to see me. Put the scattergun away, Latigo. You can go home. I'll talk to this madman and then lock up."

Roundtree was wearing a red silk robe and a pair of slippers. He came down the stairs as the bartender whipped off his apron, slammed it down on the bar, and stomped out.

"Fire that man," Trollinger said. "Nobody points a gun at me in this camp."

Roundtree had reached the foot of the stairs. He said, "Vince, you're raising hell when you've got no business doing it. I will not fire Latigo. If you had gone home as he asked you to do, he would not have pointed the shotgun at you. Now cool down, tell me what you wanted to, and then go home."

Trollinger was shaking with the violence of his anger. "I tell you to fire him." He pointed a trembling forefinger at Roundtree. "I won't stand for a man like that—"

"Vince, you're forgetting quite a few important items," Roundtree said. "I'll remind you. You want to sell out. I'm the spokesman for the buyers, me and Saul Moffat. The Denver boys will do what I say. You keep pushing like you're doing and the deal's off. Now speak your piece and get to hell out of here. I knew I didn't like you very much, but just this minute I realize I don't like anything about you."

Trollinger put a hand against the bar to steady himself. His first impulse was to knock some of Roundtree's teeth loose. He hadn't had a fight for years, but he could handle a man as soft as Roundtree. He bit his lower lip, fighting his temper until he had it under control. He could wait. Once he had completed the deal, once the papers were signed and the money in the bank, he'd come back here and make jelly out of Charlie Roundtree.

"I wanted to know about Philip Fremont," Trollinger said hoarsely.

"He's still alive." Roundtree's face was red with suppressed anger. "You didn't hear what happened?"

"No. I've been home all afternoon."

"We thought we had it all lined out," Roundtree said. "Saul and more'n a hundred men went after the kid, but Jones had some men inside the jail. I don't know how many or who they were except Judge Herald. Anyhow, they turned Saul and the crowd back." He glowered at Trollinger. "It was that Johnny Jones again. We keep underestimating him."

"Well, you've got to try again," Trollinger said, the words tumbling out of him. "Tonight. That kid has got to be strung up."

Roundtree studied Trollinger for a time, frowning. Finally he said, "There's something here that's a little off key, Vince. In fact, it's downright puzzling. This afternoon you didn't seem to care much. You just wanted Hawk taken care of."

"I still want him taken care of," Trollinger snapped. "If

104

Jones is as tough as you keep claiming he is, he'll kill Fremont as soon as Fremont starts kicking him around for letting the boy get lynched. Ain't that what you had in mind?"

"Yeah, I hoped it would work that way," Roundtree conceded, "but we couldn't pull it off, so there's other ways of handling Fremont. I intend to use those ways when he gets back or on his way back."

"No, no," Trollinger said. "It's got to be the other way. The case has got to be closed."

"Oh, so it's got to be closed," Roundtree said. "I begin to see a great light."

"I didn't mean anything by that," Trollinger said hastily. "It's just that we can't let this go, with the Fremont kid being turned loose as soon as the sheriff gets to town. You know a jury wouldn't convict him."

"Not if he's innocent," Roundtree said, "and that's what the great light tells me. You know he's innocent because you know who done it."

"Don't be a fool," Trollinger said.

"I'm sorry, Vince. We had it built up so nobody could be blamed, not when you've got a mob of a hundred men doing the lynching, but we didn't get the job done."

Trollinger's hand on the bar became a fist. He said, "You were tough with me a while ago. All right, I can be tough, too. I don't have to sell. This whole pipe dream of yours and all your fine plans can go down the drain right now if you don't hang that Fremont kid and do it tonight."

Roundtree scratched the back of his neck thoughtfully, then he said, "I guess you've got good and sufficient reasons. You want the case closed. You couldn't stand the disgrace if the truth came out, could you? That is, if I'm guessing right, and I'm pretty sure I am. All right, Vince. Go home and go to bed. It will be done."

For a moment Trollinger didn't move. He stared at Roundtree, knowing that the saloon man had guessed the truth and knowing, too, that he had just condemned an innocent boy to death. He turned and walked out of the saloon, telling himself he had done right. His responsibility was to Clay, not to Hawk Fremont's brother.

When he reached his house, it struck him that he had to tell Clay or the boy might leave the house, and someone would see the scratches and start questioning him. Clay wasn't smart enough to think of the right answers. He picked up the lamp from the desk and climbed the stairs. He opened the door of Clay's room and went in. The room was empty.

CHAPTER 20

Sunday night was the longest night Johnny had ever spent. He couldn't sleep, yet he was so tired that he felt as if he had been drugged. At times he sat beside Phil, but the boy was not inclined to talk, so Johnny would wander back into the sheriff's office and talk with the others for a minute or so, then he'd go outside and hunker down in the darkness at the edge of the light from the lamp, which made a long yellow slash against the dirt of the yard.

Age had caught up with Judge Herald. He took his Winchester, saying, "Wake me when the excitement starts," and went back to one of the cells and sprawled out on the bunk.

None of the others tried to sleep except for a minute or two at a time, when they would nod in their chairs and then wake with a start. Once, toward morning, Doc Schuman put his head down on the desk and slept for fifteen minutes. That was the longest any of them napped.

Ed Allen and Dave Royal were as restless as Johnny. They moved around, sometimes going outside and circling the jail building, then returning to look at their watches and find that only five minutes had passed.

Once Royal squatted beside Johnny, asking, "What are your plans after Hawk gets back? I know you're going to get married, but I keep hoping something will change your mind and you and Jan will stay here."

"That's one thing I'm sure I won't do," Johnny said. "I'm not sorry I came, though. I've seen a few things I'd never have seen if I'd spent my life chousing cows on the JJ. Jan and I talked about starting our own spread after we went home, but we don't have any more money than we ever had, so I'll probably wind up riding for Dad again."

"It won't do," Royal said moodily. "Not if you and Jan are going to live in the same house with your folks. I'm talking from my own experience. Yours might be different."

"I don't figure it would be," Johnny said. "We'll work something out. All we're both sure of right now is that we don't want to stay here. Jan doesn't think she's been treated right, and I know I'm not going to go on bucking men like Vince Trollinger and Charlie Roundtree. Even if I was sheriff instead of Hawk, I don't think I could change anything."

"No, you couldn't," Royal admitted. "I know how it was with Jan. She's right. She came to see my wife about making her a new dress, but Stella was ornery." He stopped, then he burst out, "Damn it, my wife is almost always ornery, but I'm stuck with her, and I don't favor divorce. She's kind of a leader among the women, and I guess none of the others had the nerve to give Jan work after Stella cut her down."

Johnny rolled and fired a cigarette, glancing at Royal as the match flame flared up and died. He was surprised. Royal kept surprising him. He had an expression of wild desperation on his face that made Johnny wonder if he would actually welcome a fight.

"I don't savvy you, Dave," Johnny said. "I figured you were the last man in camp to give me a hand. You were scared silly this morning."

"I'm still scared," Royal said. "No use denying it, but something's happened to me. I'm not sure just what it was, but . . . hell, you don't want to hear about me."

"Sure I do," Johnny said. "Like I just told you, I can't figure you out."

"I grew up scared," Royal said. "My mother insisted I was sickly, and I wasn't allowed to play rough with other boys. It wasn't true, but I never had the guts to defy her, so that was the way she raised me. I went to work in my dad's bank because Mamma didn't want me to leave home. Well, you won't believe it, but she actually picked Stella out for me to marry.

"I only remember one time after we were married that I ever gave the orders. My parents died of typhoid six years ago. I was the only child, so I fell into some money. We
107

came here because I thought that if I cut all the old connections, I'd be a different man."

Royal paused, then he said moodily, "I wasn't. Maybe a man never changes, no matter how hard he tries. Stella came here with me, though she raised hell about it. After we got here, she punished me for six months by not letting me get into bed with her. Finally I went to Antoinette's place. Stella found out and we went another six months before I had a wife."

He paused again. The sky had become overcast and the air had turned cold, with the smell and feel of rain in the air. When Royal didn't say anything for what must have been five minutes, Johnny said, "I don't think you got done."

"I'm ashamed to tell you things like this," Royal said. "I never talked to anyone about my personal life before."

"I'm interested," Johnny said. "Not that I want to pry, but for me, life was pretty simple on the JJ. We lived by the seasons, we made money according to what the price of beef was each fall, and we knew we could always make it through a bad year; but life's never simple in a mining camp. There's a dozen forces all pouring at you at the same time. I don't know why you ever picked a place like this to live."

"It was the most different from where we lived in a small farming community east of the mountains," Royal said. "That's why I thought I might be a different man, but since I've been here, I've sucked around after Vince Trollinger so he'd keep his money in my bank and not start a new one to compete with mine.

"Sure, I'm a pillar of the church, but I've never stood tough for what I believed to be right. Ed Allen's different. He can be as tough as an old boot heel when he has to. He got me to come along with him and the judge and Doc. You know, now I'm glad I came. You go just so far being scared, then you start backing up and knowing you can't get any more scared, so what the hell? You do what you can."

He laughed softly. "Johnny, you won't believe this, but I was sorry when Moffat turned and walked off. I hate that bastard and I was hoping he'd fight. I guess I wanted to kill him."

"And you don't think a man changes?" Johnny asked. "Looks to me like you've changed in the last ten, twelve hours."

"For right now I have," Royal said, "and I feel better. I'm ten feet tall. I've got a Winchester in my hands. I'll fight if we have to, but what I'm wondering about is what I'll be when I get to the bank and Trollinger starts telling me what to do. Or when I go home and my wife gives me an order."

"I'm no expert on women," Johnny said, "but maybe you ought to belt your wife one."

"It would do her a pile of good," Royal said.

The rain came in a sudden rush, sweeping down the canyon in sheets, thunder pounding above them as lightning played along both rims. Johnny and Royal went inside and shut the door. Within a matter of minutes the storm passed down the canyon, and Johnny opened the door and stood there, breathing deeply of the damp, pine-scented air.

"Be daylight in a little while and nothing's happened," Doc Schuman said. "I don't think it's going to."

"I don't think so, either," Johnny said. "If we can make it through another night, we'll be all right. From then on, it'll be up to Hawk."

"He'll take no help from us," Schuman said. "Or want it."

"What do you suppose he'll do?" Allen asked.

"I don't know," Johnny answered, "but it's my guess he'll go wild. He can't buck the whole camp, and most of the men of the camp were here this afternoon wanting to hang Phil."

"He'll try," Schuman said.

"And get strung up himself," Royal added.

"It could happen," Schuman agreed. "I can name ten men who would volunteer to put the rope on his neck. Probably I could think of more if I took a minute or two."

Johnny stepped outside, shivering a little in the chill, damp air. If the lynchers were coming, it would be in the next half hour. By that time it would be daylight.

They didn't come. Allen woke Judge Herald and told him that he and Doc Schuman and Royal were leaving. The judge said he'd better get home, too, or his wife would worry. He came out of the cell behind Allen, yawning and rubbing his eyes.

"First night in fifty years that I've slept in a jail," he said, laughing. He looked at Johnny. "I guess you were wrong again. Nobody showed up."

"I've got a perfect record," Johnny said.

"We'll keep our ears to the wind," Schuman said, "and we'll be here again tonight unless we're needed before then. I'm not sure we're out of the woods yet."

"I think we are," the judge said. "I've been through things like this, and it's been my experience that men have to be awful mad to go on a hanging party. That kind of mad wears off after a few hours."

Schuman shrugged. "We'll see. I'll drop in later this morning to see Phil."

"You ought to take a look at Annie sometime today," Johnny said.

"I'll make it a point to do that," the doctor said.

They replaced the rifles in the gunrack, Royal saying, "I'll fetch you some breakfast after while. It'll probably be an hour or more."

"No hurry," Johnny said.

They left, wading the mud to the street and crossing it, then following the boardwalk to their homes. Johnny watched them until they disappeared, his shotgun still in his hands. He felt let down. You build yourself up for the worst kind of trouble, and when it doesn't come, you feel a little empty inside. He guessed that it was that way with Dave Royal.

Johnny felt the way Royal did about Saul Moffat. The gambler had been more responsible than anyone else for the mob coming yesterday afternoon. Any man who was that anxious to hang an innocent boy deserved killing, and Johnny was sorry he hadn't had the chance to shoot Moffat.

The lynchers came then, five of them, charging around the corner of the courthouse and racing through the thin morning light toward the jail. They said nothing; they came as silently as wraiths, disguised in long yellow slickers, red bandannas over their faces, and their broad-brimmed hats pulled low over their eyes.

Johnny didn't need to be threatened or to be told what they wanted. He cocked both barrels of the shotgun as he

110

wheeled to face them, yelling, "I'll kill you if you keep coming."

Still they came, straight toward him. He didn't see any guns, but he didn't wait to find out if they were armed. He fired one barrel and saw a man go down. He hoped it was Moffat, but they all looked alike.

Without warning, the sky fell on him and he toppled forward into the mud, the other barrel going off without conscious intention on his part. Men rushed past. He struggled up on his hands and knees, the terrifying truth rushing through his numb brain. Phil would die in the next few minutes, and he was helpless to stop the lynching.

A man called, "Toss the rope over that big limb yonder."

Another said, "Don't kill him. We've got use for him."

He was struck on the head again. This time total blackness closed in. He came to later—he had no idea how much later—aware first of all that his head was about to split wide open from the skull-bursting pain; then he realized that men were running toward him, and one of them was shouting in horror, "My God, they finally did it."

He saw Phil's frail body swaying from the limb of one of the big cottonwoods that lined the courthouse block along E Street, the head cocked grotesquely to one side. Again Johnny fell forward into the mud, the blackness sweeping in all around him once more.

CHAPTER 21

For Johnny Jones the day was one of fuzzy memories, of a throbbing headache, of waking, of having Jan raise his head from the pillow to swallow a pill, of Doc Schuman feeling his head and taking his pulse, and most of all, of the horrible fear that what he had seen just before he had lost consciousness in the weeds and mud of the courthouse yard was reality and not a nightmare.

Sometime during the day he became aware that he was in Jan's bed, vaguely aware of the smell of her perfume, of her dresses hanging in the closet—which was without a door—and of her toilet articles on the marble top of the bureau.

There were times when he reached for her hand and she sat beside the bed until he went to sleep again. Neither she nor Doc Schuman tried to talk to him, and he heard nothing pass between them except the doctor's order to keep him quiet all day.

Early that evening he woke, the sharp red rays of the dying sun setting fire to the west window of his room. He was still dressed, except for his boots, which were on the floor beside the bed. His hat hung from a peg set in the wall; his gun belt was draped across a chair, under his hat.

He knew that his memory of Phil's swaying body was no nightmare. He knew, but still he had to ask, had to be sure. He sat up and swung his feet to the floor, then remained motionless for several minutes until the walls quit whirling, his teeth clenched against the crashing pain that roared through his head. He fisted his hands on his lap and sweat rolled down his face.

Presently the worst of the pain faded, and he got to his feet and walked slowly to the door. He gripped the casing until a wave of nausea passed, then he went through Jan's front room with its dressmaker's dummy and cutting table and scattering of patterns. He found her in the kitchen eating supper.

She rose when she saw him in the doorway. "How do you feel?" she asked.

"Fine," he answered. "I never felt better in my life."

"I knew you'd lie to me," she said. "I don't know why I asked you. Sit down. Doc said for you to get up this evening if you felt like it. He left some pills to make you sleep tonight. He said that if you felt all right by morning, you probably were in pretty good shape, but you'll have to stay here tonight."

He sat down at the table. "It'll ruin your reputation, having a man sleeping in your house all night."

"My reputation was ruined the day I started sewing for Antoinette and the rest of the women across the creek," she said harshly. "I certainly don't care what the good women of this camp think of me now. Besides, we'll be leaving in less than twenty-four hours."

112

"No news of Hawk?" he asked.

"Nothing," she said. "I bought a soup bone this morning after they brought you here. Doc said not to give you much to eat because you probably wouldn't keep it down today, but I've been cooking that bone since morning, and I think the broth will be good. Think you can swallow some?"

"Sure," he said. "If I make a mess—"

"I'll clean it up," she said. "Doc told me you ought to have something in your stomach tonight. That's why I quit giving you the pills. I wanted you to wake up."

She filled a bowl with broth from the kettle that was on the stove and set it in front of him, then brought a spoon and a cup of coffee. She filled her own cup and sat down across from him.

"Every minute since they brought you here I've thanked God you were alive," she said. "Doc thought that if you hadn't had your hat on, you probably would have been killed. He thinks you'll have a headache for a long time, but it will go away eventually."

The broth was hot, so he stirred it, thinking he should thank God, too, for being alive. But right now, with the mental picture of Phil dangling from the end of a rope crowding everything else out of his mind, he found it hard to be thankful for anything. He had tried to save Phil's life, but he had failed, and he would never forgive himself for that failure.

He looked up, knowing he had to ask, had to find out if there was any use to cling to the last faint hope. He asked, "Phil?"

She shook her head. "They killed him."

He shoved the bowl back. How much harder could he have tried, he thought? What else could he have done? Oh, he could have asked his four friends to stay longer at the jail. Would another hour have changed anything? Or two hours? Did the lynchers know when the four men left the jail and therefore know when he would be alone?

He sat there, staring at the broth and not seeing it. A terrible feeling possessed him that the implacable flow of destiny had washed over him and Phil and Hawk Fremont, that there was nothing he could have done that would have saved the boy's life.

"Please try to eat your broth," Jan said. "I know how

you feel and how hard you tried and how you almost got yourself killed trying to save him."

"It's done," he said. "Finished. I didn't save him."

He started to eat and succeeded in finishing the broth. He drank the coffee and put the cup down, then reached for tobacco and paper, and let his hand drop back to the table. He didn't want to smoke after all.

He heard a knock on the front door and started to get up, thinking he should have his gun, but Jan motioned for him to stay there. "It's probably Dave Royal," she said. "He was coming to see how you were."

She left the kitchen and returned a moment later with the banker. She said, "Sit down at the table with our patient, Mr. Royal. Will you have a cup of coffee?"

"It would go good," he said as he dropped into a chair, his gaze on Johnny. "How do you feel?"

"I told Jan I felt fine," Johnny said, "but I lied. It ain't just that my head aches so bad. It's letting them get Phil. I was thinking a while ago that maybe there was nothing any of us could have done."

"I was talking to Doc about it just now," Royal said. "We could have stayed with you a while longer, but we couldn't have stayed all day. We had obligations we had to take care of."

"If you had waited another hour," Johnny said, "they probably would have waited, too. They must have been watching from somewhere."

"It's my guess they waited in the courthouse," Royal said. "They could watch the jail from there. Judging from the tracks in the mud at the west door, they went out that way. Of course you wouldn't see them until they rounded the corner of the courthouse."

"But one of them slugged me from behind," Johnny said. "I never saw him at all, so he must have been hiding on the other side of the jail. How did he get there without me seeing him?"

"I'm still guessing," Royal said, "but he must have left the courthouse a minute or two before the others did. The light was still thin and you had no reason to look in that direction. Chances are he made a big circle."

"I guess that's it," Johnny agreed.

"There's another point that bothers me," Royal said thoughtfully. "They sent at least one man around the jail to knock you out. How did you have time to shoot two of them?"

"Two?" Johnny said. "I only got one."

"You killed one," Royal said. "Ed Lawler. Caught him in the throat and cut his jugular vein. Looked like a slaughterhouse. Blood all over him. You wounded the second one, the Trollinger kid. Hit him in the right leg above the knee and sure made a mess of his leg."

"Clay Trollinger?" Johnny said. "Why would he be in that bunch?"

"I sure don't know," Royal said. "I don't suppose you recognized any of the others?"

"No," Johnny answered. "They all had bandannas over their faces and wore yellow slickers, like the two you found. I had no idea who they were."

"We wondered about that," Royal said thoughtfully. "It didn't seem logical that they would leave you alive if you could identify them."

"I have a vague recollection of one of them saying not to kill me," Johnny said, "that they had use for me. Now what kind of use would a gang of lynchers have for me?"

Royal shook his head. "I don't know. You still haven't told me how or why they gave you time to shoot two of them."

"I didn't have that much time," Johnny said. "I can't remember exactly what happened. I hollered at them, but they kept coming. I do remember I shot once. It was too far for a shotgun, so I was lucky that I got Ed Lawler. That was when I was slugged the first time. The other barrel was cocked. I must have pulled the trigger as I fell and hit Trollinger by sheer good luck."

"Even so," Royal persisted, "I don't see how a plan that must have been carefully worked out would give you time to shoot even one of them."

"Something must have gone wrong with their timing," Johnny said. "That's all I know. Whoever slugged me took a few seconds more than they had allowed."

"Well, if you didn't recognize any of them," Royal said thoughtfully, "we don't know who the ones are that did the actual hanging."

"None of you saw them?"

"No, they were clean gone when we got there," Royal

said. "Doc was the first. He lives the closest. They couldn't have had much more than five minutes—ten at the outside—from the time we heard the shots. Doc cut Phil down, but we were too late. He figured you were gone, too, lying there the way you were."

Johnny stared at his hands. He said, "It took brave men to break a paralyzed boy out of jail and murder him."

"Depends on how you look at it," Royal said. "It took some guts to come at you that way, holding a scattergun in your hands the way you were."

"They didn't expect to lose anyone," Johnny said. "Not with one man delegated to knock me on the head. They must have planned it that way, thinking I wouldn't get off a shot. As early as they were, nobody else was likely to be around for half an hour or more, so they would have had plenty of time to get clear."

"How are you going at identifying the men who did it?" Royal asked.

"If Ed Lawler was in it, you can be sure Al was too," Johnny said. "You can also be sure Tim Muldoon was one of them, but I couldn't guess the other two unless one was Saul Moffat."

"Sounds like good guessing," Royal said, "but you don't convict men on guesses."

"Maybe we won't need a conviction," Johnny said.

"No. If you were Hawk Fremont, I'd say you'd shoot them down in cold blood, but you won't do that." Royal rose. "You'll arrest them and they'll get a fair trial before Judge Herald and a jury. Well, I've got to go. You take it easy."

"He will," Jan said. "He's going to bed."

Five minutes later he was back in bed, having swallowed one of the pills Doc Schuman had left. Jan bent over him and kissed him, and as she straightened, he said, "Tomorrow."

"What do you mean, tomorrow?"

"I've got four men to arrest. Or to kill if they resist arrest."

"You're not able," she cried. "You can't."

"I'll be able," he said. "I've got to do it before Hawk gets back. I liked Phil and respected him, and I know he was innocent. I can't bring him back to life, but I can take the men who murdered him."

"Johnny, Johnny," she whispered, "is this ever going to be over?"

"It'll be over by the time Hawk Fremont rides into town tomorrow afternoon," he answered.

She turned and left the room. He shut his eyes, for the moment forgetting that his head ached. He saw Phil's body hanging from the cottonwood limb, and he wondered if he would see it the rest of his life.

CHAPTER 22

Vince Trollinger had stayed up Sunday night until after midnight, hoping Clay would come in and he could talk to him about staying in the house until the scratches healed. But Clay did not come.

Trollinger had no idea where to look for the boy, so he went to bed. Still, he did not sleep. He lay in bed, listening, hoping he would hear the front door open and shut as he had so many times in the last year.

He dropped off to sleep sometime before dawn, and he felt as if he had slept only a few minutes when he was awakened by someone hammering on the front door. He sat up and felt around for his slippers; he found them and pulled them on, then staggered across the room to where he had draped his robe over the back of a chair. He slipped into it and went downstairs, still groggy and thick headed.

He opened the door to find Ed Allen standing there. He swore and would have slammed the door in the preacher's face if Allen hadn't said, "You'd better get dressed and go to Doc Schuman's house."

Trollinger had supposed Allen was after money or wanted him to do some kind of church work, but he sensed that he was wrong, that some kind of tragedy was the cause of Allen's visit. He asked, "Why?"

"A party of lynchers took Philip Fremont out of jail and hung him," Allen said. "Clay was one of the party. He was badly wounded."

Trollinger froze, unable to comprehend what he had heard. Sure, he had been hoping to hear that the Fremont boy had been lynched, but the news that Clay had been one of the lynchers was preposterous.

Charlie Roundtree was supposed to organize the lynchers, and he wouldn't include Clay. Or would he? Trollinger put a hand against the door casing, thinking that maybe Roundtree had done exactly that, perhaps out of sheer cussedness because of what Trollinger had done last night.

"I'm not surprised that the Fremont boy was lynched," Trollinger said finally, "but Clay couldn't have had anything to do with it."

"I'm afraid he did," Allen said. "You see, I was one of the first to reach the jail after Johnny Jones fired two shots trying to defend his prisoner. When I got there, Phil was dead; Ed Lawler was dead, killed by a load of buckshot; and Clay was on the ground with one leg mangled by another load of buckshot. Clay and Lawler were dressed alike in yellow slickers and bandannas covering their faces. They were lying within fifteen or twenty feet of each other."

"How bad is he?"

"Very bad," Allen said. "He lost a great deal of blood."

Of all the incredible things that could have happened, this seemed the most incredible. Finally Trollinger said, "I'll dress and go right over."

He turned and went upstairs to his room, leaving the preacher standing on the porch. He sat down on the bed, the bitterness of disappointment running through him like a corroding acid. There was simply no excuse for Roundtree including Clay in the lynch party.

No, the saloon man could have found plenty of toughs in camp to do a job like that, the Lawlers and Muldoons and even Saul Moffat. Now Clay would die and Doc Schuman and anyone else looking at his face would see the scratches and know what he had done.

Trollinger dressed and went out into the cool morning air. He felt like a hungry man who had been offered a foot-long steak perfectly cooked and then had had it snatched from him just as he reached it.

He went to the telegraph office and sent a wire to Denver saying he would accept the offer; then he walked to Doc Schuman's house, convinced the offer would be withdrawn. Charlie Roundtree had somehow turned into an enemy who was defeating him. He wasn't sure why, unless Roundtree thought he could buy all of Trollinger's property for less than the original offer.

Schuman's house was also his office. A small front room on the left was where he received his patients. Directly behind it was a larger room with a bed, where he often put his patients if they had to be nursed or required some sort of additional treatment. Clay was in this room, the blankets pulled up to his chin.

The boy lay so still and was so white that for a moment Trollinger thought he was dead. Then he bent over the bed and saw the slight movement of the blankets that covered Clay's chest. He saw, too, the red slashes down his cheek, the only color in his ghastly-white face.

Mrs. Schuman had ushered Trollinger into the room. Now she said, "The doctor would like to see you for a minute."

Trollinger nodded and followed her into the small room in front. Schuman offered his hand and Trollinger shook it, finding it hard to realize this was happening to him, that it had happened to Clay.

"Sit down, Vince," Schuman said. "I have something to ask you that has only one answer, but it's an answer you have to make. I can't do it for you."

Trollinger dropped into a rawhide-bottom chair and looked at Schuman across the desk. He did not recognize his own voice when he said, "All right, I'll give you the answer I'm supposed to."

"Clay lost a lot of blood before we got him here, where I could take care of him properly," Schuman said. "The leg is badly mangled. It should be amputated. Under ordinary circumstances I would recommend that we do it, but in his condition it is questionable whether he would survive the operation. That's the decision you have to make. Do you want me to operate?"

"No," Trollinger said. "Not if he wouldn't live through the operation. What are his chances if you don't operate?"

Schuman shrugged. "I'm too old a hand at this to give you a definite answer. The Lord gives and the Lord takes away. I don't. All I can say is, he'll live awhile." He rose. "You can stay in there with him, Vince, or you can go to your office. My wife is an excellent nurse and she will be with him most of the time. I would like for you to stay in town, where we can find you."

"I'll do that, of course," Trollinger said as he got to his feet, "but if there's nothing I can do, I won't stay." He hesitated, then he asked, "Has he talked since you brought him in?"

Schuman shook his head. "Not a word."

As Trollinger walked out of the house, he had a feeling that the doctor had been amused at the question. Schuman knew what Clay had done, so he knew, too, that there had been no reason for Philip Fremont to die.

Trollinger went to a barber shop and had a shave; then he bought his breakfast in the Bon Ton, saying nothing to Jake Norton while he was there except to give his order. He went to his office then, nodding at Ted Riley as he walked past his desk. Riley said, "Good morning, Mr. Trollinger." His tone was distant, and as Trollinger sat down in his swivel chair, he told himself that Riley might have heard about Clay, too.

The wrong boy had been lynched, and the boy who had really committed the crimes had been in the lynching party. They'd make the most out of that, he told himself, everybody from the girls and pimps across the creek on up to the preacher, Ed Allen.

He tried to work, but he couldn't keep his mind on what he was doing. He had a few letters to write and finally gave that up, too, because he couldn't even compose a rational sentence. His mind fastened on Charlie Roundtree even more than on Clay. Roundtree had proved unbelievably inept.

A man should be able to organize a lynch party at dawn when the deputy was alone and carry it to its conclusion without losing a man. But it was worse, far worse, to have included Clay. Maybe it tickled Roundtree's twisted sense of humor to have the guilty boy in the party that hung an innocent boy.

Somehow he wore out the morning. At noon he stepped into the Bon Ton and had his dinner, though he wasn't sure he could keep it down. When he walked out of the restaurant, he felt as if the last bites were still in his throat.

He returned to Doc Schuman's house and for a few

minutes sat beside the bed. There was no change in the boy's condition, Schuman said. The wound had been cleaned and dressed, the buckshot removed, and that was all that could be done. It was up to the boy now. Anyone with a young, strong body might be able to overcome the shock and loss of blood. That, Trollinger knew very well, was part of the problem. Clay had dissipated too much to have a strong body.

He returned to his office, glancing at the Belle Union across the street. He wanted a drink, and he remembered the good days when every morning he had gone into the saloon for a drink and exchanged a few pleasant words with Roundtree. He had considered the man his friend. Well, he'd know for sure sometime today when he had an answer to his wire.

The afternoon was little better than the morning. He left his desk three times to go to the telegraph office. The last time the answer was there. The offer was temporarily withdrawn. He walked back to his office, his shoulders bent, an old man.

He sat down at the desk, grunting something at Ted Riley when the man said he was going home. Trollinger had never realized before how important it was to have other people's respect. He had taken it for granted; folks were afraid to do anything else than to give him respect.

Now, after the gossip spread and everybody knew, there would be no respect for him in Pulpit Rock. His son was guilty; an innocent boy had been lynched; and Charlie Roundtree, his erstwhile friend, had cut his throat. Here were three facts he could not forget or overlook.

When it was dark, he locked the office and returned to Doc Schuman's house. He sat beside the bed for an hour, filled from head to foot with one great, throbbing ache. Trollinger did not ask Schuman or his wife about the deputy, but thought Jones had probably been informed that Clay was the one he wanted.

If Clay died, as he probably would, maybe the truth would never come out. Oh, people would know about it, all right, but maybe if it didn't come into the open, he could live here and in time even forget what had happened. But there would still be Charlie Roundtree.

Mrs. Schuman came into the room and Trollinger left. He crossed the street so he wouldn't be directly in front of the Belle Union. He found himself in front of the Bon Ton and smelled the supper they were cooking for someone, but he wasn't hungry.

For a time he stood motionless, staring at the lighted windows of the Belle Union, filled with a poison of hate he had never known before in his life. He knew, suddenly, what he had to do. He had never killed a man in his life; he had never really wanted to before.

Now he wanted to kill Charlie Roundtree, and that was exactly what he would do, because Roundtree had shot Clay as surely as if he had pulled the trigger. Even worse, he had let Trollinger dream of a million dollars and then had punctured the dream. He had claimed to be the spokesman for the Denver group, he and Saul Moffat. All right, they could accept the responsibility of being spokesman, first Roundtree and then Moffat.

CHAPTER 23

Johnny woke Tuesday morning filled with the sickening knowledge that Philip Fremont was dead. All of his thinking and talking with Dave Royal last night about how the lynching could not have been avoided did not change that one grim and terrible fact. The lynchers had succeeded in murdering an innocent and helpless boy.

Today he had work to do. For a time he lay staring at the ceiling while Jan worked in the kitchen getting breakfast. He was hardly aware of the noise Jan made or even of his headache, which was not as severe as it had been the previous morning.

He would go after Al Lawler and Tim Muldoon, since he was reasonably sure they had been in the lynching party. Muldoon probably would be in Antoinette's house as usual, but he didn't know where Lawler would hide.

The Lawler boys had lived for years in a cabin not far from the courthouse. Johnny didn't expect to find Al there, now that Ed was dead. It was always a safe bet that if one was involved in something, the other one would be too. Al would know that Johnny was bound to conclude

122

that he had been one of the lynchers. Undoubtedly, he would go into hiding somewhere.

Jan came into the bedroom and stood smiling at Johnny. She asked, "How's my future husband today?"

"I feel fine and I'm not lying as much as I was yesterday," he answered.

"Good. How about some breakfast?"

"I'm hungry," he said. "I'll be right there."

"It's almost ready," she said, and left the room.

He got up and dressed, moving slowly and carefully at first, but he found that the ache was a dull and constant one, and that the violent throbbing of the day before did not return. He went into the kitchen and washed his face and combed his hair, then sat down at the table across from Jan, who was already seated.

"This is the way it's going to be for the next fifty years," she said. "On our golden-wedding anniversary we'll have breakfast together, and you'll have a long white beard and I'll have gray hair."

"I guess so," he said, "though I hope I won't have a headache that morning."

"Do you still have it?"

"You said Doc Schuman told you I'd have it for a long time," he said. "Sure I've got it, but I feel better than I have any right to. I guess I have a thick skull."

She laughed. "Doc said something like that. A hat and a thick skull can protect a man's brain pretty well is the way he put it."

"Well, at least he admitted I've got a brain," Johnny said.

"Oh, he's broad-minded about things like that." She stared at her plate as she toyed with her bacon. Without looking at him, she asked, "What are you going to do this morning?"

"I'm going to Antoinette's house as soon as I finish eating," he answered. "I'll take Muldoon if he's there; then I'll hunt for Al Lawler, but I don't know where to start."

"I hate to have you go there alone," she said. "You need help because Al Lawler is probably hiding in one of Antoinette's upstairs rooms—the first one on the left at the head of the stairs to be exact."

He had started to reach for his coffee cup, but now he dropped his hand to the table. "How do you know?"

"I've been in and out of Antoinette's house ever since I came to Pulpit Rock," she answered. "I've been upstairs fifty times, I guess, usually fitting one of the girls, so I listen and keep my mouth shut, and I pick up quite a bit of information about them. You've seen the little blonde they call Dolly?"

Johnny nodded. "I know which one she is."

"Well, she's Al Lawler's girl," Jan said, "and Al's her solid man. They've kept it quiet because Antoinette considers it bad for business if the men of town hear that a girl belongs to a tough like Al Lawler. He hangs around the house like one of the customers and doesn't pay much attention to Dolly until the other men are gone."

Johnny thought about it a minute and decided that Jan had made a good guess, that Lawler would either leave town or hide out in some place like Antoinette's, where he thought he wouldn't be discovered.

"Do they know you know about Dolly and Al?" he asked.

"I don't think they'd make the connection," she said. "I mean, they're so used to me being there that they talk in front of me like any bunch of gossipy women. It's not likely they even remember what was said when I was there. I went over to Antoinette's place yesterday afternoon for a minute because I had to take her dress to her. It needed a little more work. I thought about Lawler hiding there, so I asked Antoinette if Dolly wanted me to make a dress for her. She had asked me just last week if I could, but I didn't have time then. Well, Antoinette acted funny and said I'd better wait a few days. She claimed Dolly was sick and staying in her room."

Johnny didn't say anything until he finished eating, then he rolled a cigarette and sat back in his chair. "I suppose they don't get up very early over there."

"They sure don't," Jan said. "Most of the girls stay in bed until noon. Muldoon cuts wood and builds a fire and cleans up the bar. They've got a Negro cook who fixes breakfast for herself and Muldoon and Percy Lamar, who's there most of the time. Antoinette and the girls straggle downstairs for breakfast any time between nine and noon."

"Muldoon probably won't expect me to come after him, so he'll probably be there," Johnny said. "I don't look for Lamar to get in my way. The judge winged him yesterday afternoon when the mob came after Phil. What about the cook?"

"Her name is Samantha," Jan answered. "She's nice. If you tell her you're not after her or the girls, I don't think she'll bother you."

He rose. "Then the sooner I get over there, the better. I might catch Lawler in bed."

He went into the bedroom and strapped his gun belt around him, then drew his .45 and checked it carefully. He had no way of knowing what to expect. With Ed Lawler shot to death and Clay Trollinger badly wounded, and both Muldoon and Al Lawler aware that Johnny Jones was alive, they might be waiting for him.

Still, it was unlikely the meeting would turn into a gun duel. If he was lucky enough to surprise them, he might be able to arrest both and throw them into jail without firing a shot. If they had any sense, they would submit to arrest because he had no real evidence against either one, but he didn't rate the intelligence of either very high.

If they were nervous enough, they'd try to fight it out. Lamar, even with a wounded arm, and the girls were imponderables. He had no choice except to play it by ear and hope the girls, including Dolly, stayed out of it.

He picked up his hat and went back to the front room, where Jan was waiting for him. She said, "Dave Royal is coming up the street. Why don't you let him go with you? It's too big a job for one man."

He kissed her, then said, "Don't worry. Give me credit for being a big enough man to handle the job."

"But Dave would help . . ." she began.

He shook his head. "Honey, you don't know how far Dave has come in the last twenty-four hours. I can't expect any more from him."

He left the cabin and waited in front for Royal, who was striding rapidly toward him along E Street. Royal called, "Good morning, Johnny. How do you feel?"

"Good, considering," Johnny answered. "Ain't you out pretty early?"

Royal grimaced. "My wife thought so. She says I've been eating too much raw meat or loco weed. If it's the meat, it's made me think I'm a hero, and if it's the loco weed, it's made me a fool. She favors the loco weed."

"You may have to belt her one yet," Johnny said.

"I'm working up to it," Royal said. "Maybe in about twenty years." He shrugged. "Doc wants to see you. He's got some news he thinks you ought to have."

"All right, you go back and tell him I'll be there in a little while," Johnny said. "I've got an errand to run first. It won't wait."

He started toward the bridge, not stopping until Royal said, "Hold on. Doc said to fetch you if you felt like walking. Otherwise he'd come to you. He said this wouldn't wait."

Johnny had reached the end of the bridge. He turned to face the banker, saying, "You tell Doc that when he starts running the sheriff's office, I'll obey his orders, but not until then. I think I know where two of the men are that we want, and I'm going after 'em before they take a notion to vamoose."

He swung around and strode across the bridge, not bothering to glance back to see if Royal was still standing there. Dave might have gone with him if he'd been asked. The banker had surprised him so much already that Johnny couldn't be sure what he would or wouldn't do.

The trouble was that in a situation like this Dave Royal might be in the way. What had happened already to the man was a minor miracle. It was stupid to expect a major one. No, this was a one-man job, and Johnny knew he had better leave it that way.

CHAPTER 24

Johnny had planned to open the front door of Antoinette's place and go in and climb the stairs; he'd kick in the door of the first room on the left at the head of the stairs, and he'd make Al Lawler a prisoner before the man knew what was happening. When Johnny reached the front porch, he stopped. Someone was chopping wood

126

behind the house. If Jan was right, the wood chopper would be Tim Muldoon.

For a time Johnny hesitated, considering his choices. He could still go ahead as planned, but once he took Ed Lawler prisoner, Muldoon would be warned and he'd make a run for it. On the other hand, if he arrested Muldoon quietly, there was a chance he could get him to jail without waking everyone in the house; then he could return for Lawler.

He was very much aware that he was gambling against long odds, but the chance seemed worth taking. Too, he had a hunch that Muldoon was a tougher man than Lawler, and it would be safer to take him first.

Stepping off the porch, he circled the house, moving slowly and keeping below the windows so he wouldn't be seen if anyone in the house was awake and in one of the rooms on this side. When he had nearly reached the back corner of the house, he pulled his gun, cocked it, and slipped around the corner, then stopped. No one was in sight.

The ax leaned against the chopping block and a pile of stove-length wood was on one side. Muldoon must have just finished and gone into the kitchen. Johnny eased forward toward the back door, which opened from the kitchen onto a small porch. The door was open and he heard Muldoon grumble, "I'm hungry. Why ain't you got breakfast ready, you black bitch?"

"Don't you black bitch me," a woman cried, "and you git outta them doughnuts afore I bang your head with a frying pan. They're for the girls, not a big ugly like you."

There was more talk that Johnny couldn't follow. He had no idea whether Muldoon would return to the woodpile or not, but he didn't want to try to arrest the man in the kitchen. There might be shooting, and he didn't want to risk injuring the cook. He had almost made up his mind to return to the front and follow his original plan when he heard Samantha say, "Fetch in the rest o' that wood. I ain't gonna tote it in here like I done yestiddy. It's your job and you do it."

The front door bell rang. Muldoon said, "Go see who's out there."

"You go git that wood," Samantha said. "And stay outta them doughnuts."

Johnny eased back toward the corner of the house as Muldoon crossed the kitchen in his heavy-footed gait; he came through the door, crossed the porch, and stepped to the ground before Johnny said, "Hook the moon, Muldoon. You're under arrest."

Muldoon reacted faster than Johnny had thought it was possible for him to move. He whirled to face Johnny, drawing his gun as he turned. "Drop it," Johnny shouted.

Muldoon may have panicked. Or he may have made up his mind he'd rather die being arrested than hang. In any case, he completed his turn and had his gun almost level when Johnny fired. The bullet caught the big man in the chest and jolted him back a step and half around, but he did not go down.

He was dying on his feet, but he had fixed his stubborn mind on one thing: to kill Johnny Jones, who had slugged him with a gun barrel in the street Sunday afternoon. He did not drop his gun, but it sagged in his hand, so when he used the last of his great strength to pull the trigger, the slug drove into the ground halfway between him and Johnny.

Muldoon's knees buckled and he collapsed like a great tent when the guy ropes are cut one by one. He toppled forward, face down in the litter of chips around the chopping block.

Al Lawler! Johnny ran forward, knowing the man would be warned. Still, he might be surprised if he thought he was safely hidden. Johnny raced through the kitchen and on through the dining room. Reaching the hall, he stopped, stunned by surprise. Dave Royal stood just inside the door, holding a gun on Samantha, Percy Lamar, and Antoinette, who was in her nightgown.

When Antoinette saw Johnny, she screamed, "You bastard! I'll kill you for this. When Hawk gets back, he'll—"

"Hold 'em right there, Dave," Johnny said, and ran up the stairs, taking two of them at a time.

He reached the hall and glanced along it. Some of the doors were open and several girls in nightgowns were peeking out cautiously to see what was happening. Johnny

128

whirled to face the first door to his left. He had no time to think about this, although he knew that if Lawler had the guts to make a fight out of it, the man might smoke him down before he had a chance to shoot. The one thing he could not afford to do was to give Lawler time.

He kicked the door in and lunged through it and to one side, his gaze sweeping the room. The bed was mussed up, and the little blonde named Dolly was cowering in a corner, white-faced and completely naked. She was bent forward, her hands between her legs as if trying to cover herself with them. All the time she was screaming steadily in a high-pitched tone that seemed to go on and on as if she had no need to pause for breath.

Johnny wheeled and ran out of the room, pausing again in the hall. Doors slammed shut. Antoinette called from the foot of the stairs, "Come down here, you stinking son of a bitch. No men are allowed up there in the morning."

Time was still the answer to his problem, Johnny thought. The window at the back of the hall was open. Two hands were visible, clutching the sill. Lawler must have run out of the room when he heard the shots and crawled through the window, and now he was hanging there, hoping to scramble back as soon as Johnny left. The trick was to get him to stay where he was.

"Dave," Johnny called, "I think he's hiding downstairs, but you watch the hall. If he's in one of these rooms, he might try to make a run for it. If he does, kill him."

Johnny ran down the stairs, his gun still in his hand, ignoring the curses that the red-faced Antoinette screamed as he went past her. He lunged through the back door, jumped off the porch, and looked up. Al Lawler, clad in his underclothes, still dangled from the window.

"You're a pretty sight, Al," Johnny said. "Now just let go and drop. If you start scrambling back inside, I'll shoot you."

Lawler hesitated, looking down at Johnny and the revolver that was in his hand; then he let go and dropped to the ground. He hit hard, sprawling on his back, grunting and cursing. He slowly rolled over and sat up, then began to curse again, stopping only when Johnny said, "Get up. You're going to jail." He raised his voice to yell, "Come on, Dave. I've got him."

Lawler struggled to his feet, shaken up enough by his fall to reel a little. Johnny understood how it was with him. When Ed was alive, the Lawler twins were considered tough hands, but they had backed each other. Now that Al was alone, there was nothing tough about him.

Royal came out through the back door, saw Muldoon's body, and turned away from it, the corners of his mouth working. He said, "This job gets meaner all the time."

"That's right, and we've still got two to go," Johnny said as he motioned to Lawler. "Move."

"Barefooted?" Lawler howled. "Right through town?"

"Barefooted and in your underclothes right down E Street to the jail," Johnny said. "If you want to argue with me about it, remember one thing. I was conscious long enough to see Phil hanging from that limb. That was all I needed to make me want to kill the six of you, so give me an excuse and I will."

Lawler stared at him for a moment, then realized that Johnny meant exactly what he said. The frightened man turned and started toward the bridge. Antoinette had followed Royal, and now she yelled, "I'll get you for this, Jones. I'll get you as sure as—"

He turned back. "Shut up and listen to me. You were hiding two men wanted by the law. I think you'll go to jail for that. If you keep yelling at me, I know you will."

That was enough to shut her up. Johnny caught up with Royal, the two of them pacing a few steps behind the red-faced Al Lawler. Johnny asked, "How'd you get into the game and where did you get the gun? I didn't know you'd started packing one."

"I haven't," Royal said. "I mean, I'm not. Oh, hell." He glanced obliquely at Johnny. "You might as well know. Jan figured you'd need help and she gave me the gun."

"Keep it," Johnny said angrily. "Jan don't need it if she's going to give it away." They crossed the bridge and went on along E Street past Jan's place. She stood in the doorway and waved at them, but Johnny ignored her, telling himself that once he had Lawler safely locked up, he'd come back and take this up with Jan.

Royal said nothing until after they crossed the intersection of Main and E Streets. Several people who saw the procession stopped to stare and some laughed. A couple of small boys jeered at Lawler. He went on, picking his way carefully.

As they started across the courthouse yard to the jail, Royal said, "I know I wasn't much help, Johnny, but I like myself a lot more this morning than I did at this time yesterday morning. Or any other morning I can remember. I still don't know what happened to me, but I feel like a man who has just come out of a dark cave."

"I'm not blaming you," Johnny said quickly. "It took guts to go in there the way you did . . ." He stopped, realizing that if Percy Lamar or Antoinette had been free, one of them could have shot him in the back. "I'm wrong, Dave. If it hadn't been for you and Jan, I might be dead by now."

"I thought I was some help," Royal said with pardonable pride.

CHAPTER 25

For the second day in a row Vince Trollinger was awakened in the morning by someone pounding on his front door. Again he put on his slippers and robe and staggered down the stairs. He was as stiff and sore as if he had been in a hard fight. Never in his life had he felt like an old man, but he did now.

He opened the door and discovered that it was the preacher again. He swore, then asked sullenly, "What do you want now, Parson?"

Allen looked at him as if he were sorry for him. He said, "Clay's conscious and sent for me. Doc thought you'd want to be there too."

"Is he . . . is he dying?"

"I don't know," Allen said. "I don't suppose Doc knows. Clay says he wants to make a statement, so I would guess he believes he is."

Trollinger took a long breath. He had never been so tired in his life. It wasn't the physical kind of fatigue that he had experienced when he was climbing the canyon walls with a burro, trying to find the source of the rich chunks of float he had picked up along the creek. No, this was a different tiredness, a hopeless feeling that he had no future, that he had simply come to the end of the trail.

"I'll get dressed and come right down," he said.

"I'll wait for you," Allen said. "We can walk to Doc's house together. I've got something I want to say."

"If you're trying to save my soul again . . ." Trollinger began belligerently.

"No," Allen said.

Trollinger eyed him truculently, then he said, "Come in," and turned and climbed the stairs.

He dressed slowly, wondering what Clay would say in his statement. Would he admit that he had killed and robbed Mrs. Engel and had raped the girl? Surely not. Let that damned Johnny Jones think what he wanted to. He couldn't prove anything just from a scratch on Clay's cheek.

Trollinger finished and looked at himself in the mirror. His eyes were bloodshot, his face was puffy, his stubble made him look like a tramp. He had not slept much the night before. His mind had been on Charlie Roundtree, not Clay. He could not understand—even after the saloon man's duplicity had become so clear—how it had happened, but his determination to kill Roundtree did not waver.

It was not a rational decision, but nothing in his life for the last few days had been rational. That was the hardest part of all to understand, how a life as satisfactory and well ordered as his could, within a matter of hours, turn into complete anarchy.

The last thing he did before he left his bedroom was to take his short-barreled .38 from a bureau drawer, check the action, see that the cylinder carried five loads, and then slip the gun under his waistband. When he went down the stairs, he found Allen sitting in the parlor waiting.

"I'm ready," Trollinger said as he took his black derby off the hall rack and clapped it on his head.

They went out into the chill morning air, Trollinger's eyes sweeping the aspen-covered canyon walls. He said, "We're getting quite a bit of color the last day or two," and wondered why he said it.

"Yes, we are." Allen cleared his throat. "These are terrible days, Mr. Trollinger. The evil things that have happened, of course, are the culmination of the months and years of taking evil too lightly in Pulpit Rock. We are simply reaping what has been sowed. The unfortunate part of the whole thing is that innocent people suffer in the reaping."

Trollinger clenched his teeth. He was in no mood to listen to a sermon this morning. He had no affection whatever for Ed Allen, whom he considered a very young man, a pip-squeak just out of seminary taking his first church here in Pulpit Rock. The only reason Trollinger had ever given a nickel to the church since Allen came was that he had always made a token gift and he hadn't stopped, though he had made up his mind that he would.

All the preachers before Allen's time had preached about heaven and hell and other proper spiritual matters, but this loudmouth went off on such tangents as safety devices in the mine and long hours and gambling and brothels and similar subjects he had no business mentioning from the pulpit.

"I am not taking this walk to hear you—" Trollinger began.

"I know," Allen interrupted, "but I think you had better listen. You see, Clay may not die, and if he lives, he faces the same future that Philip Fremont faced. If not for his part in Philip's death, then certainly for the murder of Mrs. Engel."

"He didn't have nothing to do with that," Trollinger said loudly—too loudly he realized as soon as he had said it. "What are you trying to do, Allen?"

"I think you know," Allen said quickly, "but we're almost there, and I haven't got around to what I wanted to say. I've spent some time at the boy's bedside, and I've talked to Doc Schuman about him. The wound he received was not one that would always prove fatal. I mean, it is painful and he did lose a great deal of blood and his whole system was disturbed, of course, but this is not always enough to make a man die."

"Damn it," Trollinger said angrily, "that's not the way Doc talked yesterday."

"Now let me finish," Allen said. "The trouble has been something that Doc or nobody else could put his finger on. It has to do with the will to live. Clay has not wanted to live. Along with these other things I have mentioned, the desire to die is enough to kill him."

"Hogwash," Trollinger said sullenly. "You don't will to live or die. You do whichever comes to you."

"No, you're quite wrong about that, Mr. Trollinger," Allen said. "Of course if a man is shot through the head, he dies, but if it is a touch-and-go thing like this is, his attitude can decide what happens."

"I still don't savvy what you're getting at," Trollinger said. "If he's going to hang, he'd better die right there in Doc Schuman's bed."

They reached the doctor's house and turned up the path to the front door. Trollinger felt the preacher's gaze on him and he resented it. Preachers seemed to figure they had a special pipeline to God. Well, he didn't believe it.

Maybe he was indifferent to Clay's fate, but why should he be anything else after all the hell the boy had raised? Now, to cap everything, he had let himself be involved in a lynch party, and that gave Roundtree an excuse to see that the Denver men withdrew their offer.

"I feel sorry for you, Mr. Trollinger," Allen said, "but I feel much sorrier for your son. I had hoped at this time you could find a little love in your heart for him, a little tenderness."

They reached the front door. Trollinger opened it, then turned to Allen, his fists clenched. He wanted to hit the preacher, to knock some of that sanctimonious, holier-than-thou attitude out of him, but Allen didn't even glance at him. He walked past him along the hall and into the room where Clay lay in bed.

Trollinger followed, breathing hard and wishing he was anywhere but here. Doc Schuman and Judge Herald were in the room, Herald holding a writing tablet in one hand and a pencil in the other. Clay was on his back, as pale as he had been the day before. He looked at Trollinger briefly, then at Allen.

"How do you feel?" Trollinger asked when he reached the side of the bed.

"How does anyone feel when he's dying?" the boy said. "Mr. Allen, I'm going to make my dying statement to the judge. I'm scared. I never really thought about dying or about what it means. Do you think I'll go to hell?"

"I have nothing to do with that," Allen said. "The final

judgment is up to God. You know what your life has been."

"Yeah, I know," Clay said hopelessly. "If it depends on that, I'll roast in hell forever, but I got to thinking that if I told everything I know, it might help."

"Don't admit nothing," Trollinger warned. "You're not dying. If they think you've done something wrong, let them prove it."

"Shut up," Clay said. "What about it, Mr. Allen? Would it help?"

"Yes, Clay," Allen answered. "I think it will."

"You ready, Judge?" Clay said. "Go ahead with the questions if you are."

"All right," the judge said. "Give me your full name."

"Clayton Trollinger."

"You are in full command of your senses?"

"Yes, but I know I'm dying."

"You swear before God to answer truthfully anything I ask you to the best of your ability?"

"Yes."

"All right. Now, did you murder Mrs. Engel?"

"Yes."

"Tell us about what happened."

"I had to have money to pay a gambling debt to Charlie Roundtree. My father wouldn't give it to me. I knew Mrs. Engel had taken four hundred dollars out of the bank. Late Saturday night I stole a pillowcase off the line back of the Fremont place. I cut eyeholes in it, put it on, and went into the Engel house. I began hunting for the money in Mrs. Engel's bedroom. She woke up just as I found it. She yanked the pillowcase off my head. I killed her because she recognized me and I was afraid she would have me arrested."

"Did you rape Annie Engel?"

"No. She ran into the room and tried to hold me. I pushed her away and tore her nightgown and ran out of the house through the back door."

"Now about the lynch party that hung Philip Fremont. How did you get involved in that?"

"I left the house Sunday night and went to the Belle Union to get a drink. Charlie Roundtree took me into the back room and got me into a poker game with the Lawlers and Tim Muldoon. I drank too much. Later that night

Roundtree came in and said I had to go with them. They were going to hang Philip Fremont and then the case would be closed and I wouldn't have to worry any more. He said he knew I murdered Mrs. Engel and this was the only way I could save my own neck."

"How did he know you murdered Mrs. Engel?"

"He saw the scratches on my face, but I think it was mostly something my father had said or done earlier that night. He insisted on Phil being lynched. Roundtree said my father was the one who talked about the case being closed. Roundtree told me my father couldn't stand the disgrace of having everyone know his son had murdered Mrs. Engel."

"That's a lie!" Trollinger shouted hoarsely. "Nothing but a goddamn lie. I didn't want Clay involved in the lynching. The whole thing's Roundtree's fault."

Judge Herald ignored him. "All right, Clay. Who else participated in the hanging besides you and Ed Lawler?"

"His brother Al, Muldoon, Moffat, and Roundtree."

"What happened that made it go wrong? I mean, what gave the deputy enough time to shoot two men? Wasn't it planned better than that?"

"I don't know what went wrong, but Roundtree had it planned down to the exact second. Muldoon wanted to be the one who slugged Jones because Jones had slugged him in the street Sunday afternoon. We waited in the courthouse and watched the jail until the four men left. Muldoon made a wide circle so he could get behind Jones, but it took him too long. Roundtree thought he gave Muldoon all the time he'd need. Muldoon had been drinking. Maybe that was the reason it didn't work right."

"Where did they hide afterward? We didn't see any of them when we got there."

"It didn't take long to hang Phil, I guess," Clay answered. "The plan was to go to the Lawler cabin as soon as they finished and leave the slickers there. With everyone excited and running to the courthouse and cutting Phil down, they figured no one would notice them drift back to wherever they'd naturally be in the morning. Besides, Roundtree had two women in the Belle Union who were going to swear that all of us were in the saloon during the hanging."

136

Trollinger couldn't stand it any longer. "Why am I here to listen to this?" he demanded, staring at Allen. "Are you trying to get me involved in a crime I had nothing to do with?"

Herald looked at him. "Can you think of anyone who had more to do with Philip Fremont's death than you did? Or, setting that aside for a moment, aren't you in the least concerned about your son?"

Trollinger apparently heard only the first question. "I had nothing to do with it," he shouted hysterically. "Nothing! I'm not staying here to listen to any more of these lies."

He lunged past Allen into the hall and ran out of the house. He kept running until he was short of breath and could not run any more. Why had Allen dragged him into Clay's confession? Why? Why? Why?

CHAPTER 26

When Johnny reached Doc Schuman's house, Ed Allen met him at the door and motioned for Johnny to follow him. He moved along the hall to the room where Clay Trollinger lay in bed. The preacher nodded at the boy, who lay motionless on his side, his back to Johnny. His face was very pale, but his breathing was steady. Apparently he was asleep.

Johnny turned to Allen, not sure what he was supposed to do or say. He opened his mouth, then closed it when Allen put his fingers to his lips. He turned back to look more closely at young Trollinger, noting for the first time that there was an expression of peace on his face that Johnny had never seen before. In the past he had been filled with resentment, anger, and rebellion every time Johnny had seen him.

When Johnny swung back to face Allen, the preacher motioned him into Schuman's office. He stepped through the doorway and saw that the doctor and Judge Herald were sitting there, Schuman at the desk and Herald across from him, his chair canted back against the wall.

Allen came in and shut the door. He said, "Clay's

sleeping quietly enough now." He nodded at Johnny. "Did you notice anything about his face? I mean besides being pale as it naturally would be."

Johnny studied the preacher a moment, then he said, "I don't know yet what you're getting at, but it's the first time I ever saw him when he didn't look like he was mad at everybody and wanting to fight."

"That's exactly what I mean," Allen said. "The threads that make up the designs of human behavior are all mixed up. You see, Clay's been lying there unconscious most of the time since the—"

"I'm not sure about that, Ed," Schuman broke in. "He may have been shamming. I think he knew his goose was cooked, and he figured he didn't want to see or talk to anybody. Of course he is weak from the loss of blood and he was in a state of shock, not only from the wound but from all that's been happening, and what he knew damned well was ahead of him if he lived."

"Anyway, he decided he wanted to see me," Allen said, "mostly, I suppose, because I was the only preacher in town. I fetched his father because I thought he ought to be here if Clay made a confession. Of course I didn't know what the boy was going to say, but I had a hunch he might confess. It seems he thought he was dying and he's made up his mind that he will."

"Dying in bed is better than hanging," Herald said. "It's like Doc said a while ago. Clay knows he faces a rope if he lives."

Allen nodded. "I suppose so. Anyhow, he got worried about his immortal soul and thought that if he made a statement, God would forgive his sins. Well, all I've got to say is that God has a lot to forgive him for. Any previous time when Clay was perfectly healthy and I'd ask him to come to church, he'd laugh in my face."

"So would Vince," the judge said. "The truth is, Clay has a lot of his dad's attitudes, but I guess Vince wouldn't admit that."

"No, he sure wouldn't," Allen said. "It's hard to imagine any boy doing more evil than Clay has in his short life, but that's neither here nor there. I'm just glad I'm not God, who has to do the judging."

"Here's the statement Clay made," Herald said, handing Johnny the sheets of paper upon which he had writ-

138

ten the questions he had asked and the answers Clay had given. "We thought you'd want to read it before you went any further. It clears up several things."

Johnny read the questions and answers and gave the sheets back to the judge. "So Clay was the one who murdered Mrs. Engel and then joined the lynch party to hang Phil," he said bitterly. "Ed, for a little while I'd like to be God just to judge that bastard."

"At least you know who the six are," Herald said.

"Muldoon is dead and Al Lawler is in jail," Johnny said. "Now I'm going after Moffat and Roundtree."

"Wait a minute," Allen said. "They're not going anywhere, and you know where to find them when you want them. It's Vince Trollinger I'd like to see brought to justice."

"I sure don't savvy you this morning, Ed," Johnny said. "I don't know of any law he's broken. I said before, he wouldn't give us any help, but that don't make him a criminal. Just a damn poor citizen."

Allen looked at his hands, which were clenched on his lap. He started to say something and choked. A pulse was pounding in his temples, and when he raised his head to look at Johnny, he was trembling.

"Johnny, it's wrong to hate anybody," Allen said in a low tone. "Particularly for me. I try to live what I preach, but right now I don't seem able to. In spite of anything I can do, I hate Vince Trollinger. Oh, I know that Charlie Roundtree has been the leader of the tough element, and Hawk Fremont never did a thing to really remedy the situation. We've all heard the gossip that Fremont takes ten per cent of the profit from the saloons and brothels, and that Zero Moran is his payoff man, so that Fremont wouldn't be involved personally."

The preacher paused, apparently not sure he should pursue this. Johnny said, "Go on, Ed. I still can't see that you're convincing me I should arrest Trollinger."

Allen shook his head. "I guess that's the whole trouble. It's like you say. As far as we know, he's not a criminal. Of course you can't do anything about him just because of the injustice of what's happening and will happen to Clay."

"Clay's got to be responsible for his own crimes," Johnny said. "His father ain't responsible for them."

Allen got up and walked to the window, then whirled to face Johnny. "I think he is. Sure, Clay is the one who faces the rope, but I say Vince Trollinger is the one who should hang. He could have cleaned this camp up any time he wanted to. Instead, he did nothing. He drank with Roundtree and played poker with him and patronized the brothels. Everybody in the camp knows that."

Johnny shook his head. "Ed, looks to me like the preacher's showing in you. All mining camps have saloons and brothels. In a way, Hawk has given us pretty good law enforcement. I don't think there's a crooked poker game or rigged wheel in the saloons, and I never have heard any complaints about men being drugged and rolled in the brothels. That happens in some camps, you know."

"Sure, I know that," Allen said impatiently. "Out of one side of my head I know that everything you just said is true, but out of the other side of my head I hate the man because of what he could have been and could have done, owning most of the town the way he has. Instead, he's the most self-centered man I ever met."

Allen threw out a hand toward the room where Clay was in bed. "That's what makes me really furious. Trollinger's wife died when the boy was young. He let his housekeepers raise Clay. All that Trollinger ever did was to give him anything and everything he wanted. On the other hand, if he had given Clay something worthwhile— a little love, a little understanding—Clay would have been a different boy."

Johnny rose. "I agree with all you say about Trollinger, but I still say there's nothing I can do about him. Maybe being a bad father ought to be a crime, but we don't have any law like that on the books, do we, Judge?"

"No," Herald said, "we sure don't."

"I know I've been talking like a fool," Allen said, "but it seems to me that Trollinger's getting off scot-free and there is no justice in it."

"I'm not sure he will get off scot-free," Doc Schuman said thoughtfully. "For one thing, the crimes Clay has committed have hurt Vince. For another thing, and I've seen this happen more than once, fate or destiny or whatever you want to call it has a way of stepping in and seeing that justice is done."

"You're a bunch of philosophers today," Johnny said, unable to keep a note of impatience out of his voice, "but it's my job to do something about Saul Moffat and Charlie Roundtree, and I'm going to do it right now."

He hesitated, wondering if any of them would offer to help. To tackle two men as tough as Roundtree and Moffat—and maybe a bartender like Latigo to boot—was too much for one man. But they said nothing. They looked at him and nodded agreement that it was his job. Even Ed Allen, wrapped up in his moral indignation the way he was, said nothing about going into the Belle Union with him.

He left the doctor's house, knowing he was alone again, just as much alone as he had been Saturday afternoon when Hawk Fremont and Zero Moran had ridden out of town. As he walked slowly toward Main Street, the thought struck him that Dave Royal would have gone with him if he had been in the doctor's office. The idea would have been preposterous on Sunday morning, but it wasn't preposterous now.

Johnny drew his gun and checked it before he reached Main Street, realizing that luck would have a part in this. He would have to keep the bartender in sight. Moffat, he judged, was the more dangerous of the two men. He'd pull his gun and make a fight out of it when Johnny told him he was under arrest, but Roundtree was the sly kind who would fire a derringer from his pocket if he was close enough, or shoot Johnny in the back if he had a chance.

Johnny had not quite reached the corner when he heard two shots. They were close together, so close that the second almost seemed to be an echo of the first. He started to run, the thought coming to him that maybe by sheer accident, or through what Doc Schuman called fate or destiny, justice had come to Vince Trollinger.

When he reached Main Street, he saw no evidence of what might have been a gun fight. Jake Norton had stepped out of the Bon Ton to see what the row was about, and Jasper Hicks appeared in the archway of the livery stable. Johnny didn't think that either knew what had happened; then he saw Rolly Poe coming toward him, lurching as if he were drunk.

Johnny ran to meet him, doubting that even Rolly Poe

141

could be this drunk so early in the morning. When Johnny reached him, he demanded, "What happened?"

Poe pointed back along the street. He started to say something, but he couldn't get a word out. He wasn't drunk at all, Johnny saw. He was just plain scared.

"Where?" Johnny asked, thinking Rolly could tell him that much at least.

"Belle Union," Poe managed.

Johnny ran past him toward Roundtree's saloon, thinking that he should have known.

CHAPTER 27

Trollinger leaned against the front wall of the livery stable, struggling to suck breath back into his tortured lungs. He wasn't Vince Trollinger who owned the Queen of Sharon mine and the mill and most of the town of Pulpit Rock, Vince Trollinger who for years had been respected and treated with great courtesy—almost reverence—Vince Trollinger who had only to snap his fingers at any man in camp and order that man to do something and have it done.

He didn't know who he was, but he did know he had been to the mountain top and had been promised he could have all he could see, but it had been an empty promise, an illusion. He had a son who was an admitted murderer and thief and maybe a rapist even though he denied it, a son who could either die in bed where he lay or hang if he recovered.

He wiped away the sweat that was running down his cheeks, aware that Jasper Hicks had stepped through the archway and was staring at him; then he heard the livery-man ask, "Is there anything I can do for you, Mr. Trollinger?"

"No," Trollinger said curtly. "Just let me alone."

Hicks disappeared inside the stable. Trollinger hated him. He hated his own son for the disgrace he had brought down upon him. He hated Ed Allen for taking him to Doc Schuman's house to hear Clay's confession. He hated Schuman and Judge Herald for wringing that confession out of Clay. Why couldn't they let the boy alone, just let him die?

He wiped the sweat away once more, and then it came to him that hate was a relative thing. His world had tumbled down around him, but these were not the people who had brought it down. Charlie Roundtree was the man responsible for all that had happened. Trollinger had promised himself he would kill Roundtree, and now he wondered why he hadn't done it. If he hadn't been given sufficient reason before, he had been now.

He dropped his right hand to his side and felt the revolver he had slipped under his waistband. It was still there. He took a long breath and started walking toward the Belle Union. He staggered a little, finding that his legs did not respond to their mental orders in quite the way they should.

It didn't make any difference now what happened, and he could not undo anything that had happened in the past. All he could do was to see that Charlie Roundtree got what he deserved.

Trollinger paused outside the bat wings to wipe his face again. He moistened his lips, tasting the salty sweat that had dried on them; then he pushed back the swinging doors and went inside. The sour smell of alcohol came to him, and a little later he caught the fragrance of Saul Moffat's Havana.

Latigo was behind the bar, staring at him with cold dislike. The barfly Rolly Poe stood talking to Latigo, probably trying to work him for a drink. Moffat sat at a poker table to Trollinger's right. He was shuffling a deck of cards, his cigar tipped at a jaunty angle, his gaze on Trollinger as if not knowing what to expect.

Rolly Poe turned to stare at him, then he stood motionless. None of them spoke. Charlie Roundtree was not in sight. He was probably in the back room. Trollinger strode along the bar, bellowing, "Roundtree, where the hell are you?"

Moffat called, "Hold it, Vince."

Trollinger stopped. The door to the back room opened and Roundtree came through it, as well groomed and urbane as ever. He said, "Good morning, Vince. What brings you out so early?"

Then Roundtree stopped, his gaze fixed on Trollinger's

face; and for the first time in the years that Trollinger had known him, he actually looked frightened.

"I'll tell you what got me out so early, Charlie," Trollinger said. His lips were stiff and dry, his voice did not sound right to him, and once more he had that strange feeling of not knowing who he was. "Ed Allen got me out of bed and took me to Schuman's house. Clay's still alive. Judge Herald took his statement. Now they all know what he did."

"I'm sorry about that, Vince, but I . . ."

"You're going to be sorrier." Trollinger stood ten feet from him, but now he took three long strides, so that he was very close to Roundtree. "You're to blame for everything that has happened to Clay and me and Phil Fremont."

"Now hold on," Roundtree said sharply. "You're the one who pushed me into—"

Trollinger's right fist lashed out and caught Roundtree in the mouth, a powerful sledging blow that knocked the saloon man against the wall. He bounced off and fell, then lay motionless on his side, a hand gingerly touching his bruised and bloody lips.

"I'm going to kill you," Trollinger said, "for what you've done to me and to Clay."

His right hand swept his gun up from his waistband, he saw Roundtree raise an arm as if to ward off the bullet, he heard the saloon man cry out, "No, Vince, no."

Something hit him in the side before he could level his gun, a great numbing blow that slammed him against the bar. He pulled the trigger of his revolver as he fell, the bullet going wild. One hand reached out to grasp the brass foot rail at the base of the bar. He saw Roundtree get to his feet; he saw Moffat circle till he was in front of him, watching him closely, his smoking gun in his hand.

"The bastard's out of his head," Roundtree said. "He really aimed to kill me."

"He aimed to, all right," Moffat said. "I held off as long as I could."

Latigo was standing beside them then, all three staring down at him as if puzzled by what he had tried to do. Their voices sounded faint; they appeared to be floating uncertainly in the air. All three were very tall and thin, too, even Roundtree, who was a little on the fat side. A

144

strange gray cloud surrounded them. He wondered if the cloud distorted them, and how it got there, inside the saloon.

Someone was kneeling beside him, asking, "Who did it?"

Jones! Trollinger couldn't see his face clearly, but it sounded like the deputy, Johnny Jones. Trollinger said, "Roundtree. He did all of it. He's the one who should hang, not Clay."

The cloud moved toward him, obscuring Jones's face. Now it was black, deadly black. It picked him up and carried him away, and then the blackness was in front of him and in him and finally all around him.

CHAPTER 28

Vince Trollinger was dead. Johnny rose and for a few seconds stood looking down at the body. Trollinger was no longer the great power in Pulpit Rock. He would never again walk down Main Street as if he owned everyone and everything in camp; he would never again give an order to anybody.

Now, gazing at his face with its staring eyes and the mouth that had sagged open, its corners red from the trickles of blood, Johnny had the same feeling of deep anger that Ed Allen had expressed a few minutes before. This man, who could have done so much, had been nothing.

"It was self-defense, Deputy," Moffat said.

"That's right," Roundtree added. "He came in here to kill me."

"They're absolutely right," Latigo said. "I saw what happened. He was crazy as a hoot owl when he came in. I've seen mad dogs that had the same look in their eyes he had."

"He hit me and knocked me down," Roundtree went on. "Feels like he loosened a couple of teeth. He had no excuse. He just hauled off and let me have it. After I was down, he pulled his gun and was aiming to kill me."

They could be telling the truth or they could be lying to

clear each other. Johnny had no way of knowing. It didn't make much difference either way, because it had nothing to do with Phil Fremont's killing. They were guilty of that regardless of the facts concerning Trollinger's death, but he wanted to know the truth just for the record. He would tell Hawk Fremont when he rode in this afternoon, though Hawk might not care any more than Johnny did.

He turned to Latigo. "Give me your sawed-off shotgun."

"Oh no," Latigo said. "It stays right where it is. When I need it, I need it bad."

"Lay it on the bar," Johnny said, "or I'll come after it."

"Do what he says," Roundtree ordered.

Latigo cursed, glancing at Moffat, who stood against the wall across the room from Johnny. The gambler's gun was in his holster, and his eyes were fixed on Johnny, his right hand close to the walnut butt of his revolver.

Slowly Latigo stooped, picked up the shotgun, and laid it on the cherry-wood bar. Johnny broke it, extracted the shell, and tossed the shotgun into a corner. He glanced again at Moffat. The gambler had not moved a muscle. He was trying to say, Johnny thought, that he would not be taken alive.

"Stay where you are, all three of you," Johnny said, and turned to the door.

A crowd had gathered in front of the Belle Union, but it was a subdued crowd, nothing like the unruly mob Johnny had faced in the street when Philip had been thrown from his horse, or the crowd in front of the jail when Johnny had faced Moffat and Judge Herald had shot Percy Lamar.

The tough element was missing. These were the ordinary honest men of Pulpit Rock who carried on the camp's business, Jake Norton and Jasper Hicks and others. Dave Royal was running toward the Belle Union from E Street. These men would not interfere; they had been chastened by the lynching. After a night's sleep, they were probably glad their hands were not stained by Philip Fremont's blood.

Johnny's gaze swept the crowd until he saw Rolly Poe standing in the back. He called, "Rolly, come here."

Poe hesitated, plainly wanting no part of this, but he

lacked the courage it took to disobey Johnny's order. He shuffled forward, mumbling, "I didn't have nothing to do with nothing that happened."

Dave Royal shouldered through the crowd. When he reached Johnny, he asked, "Can I help?"

Johnny hesitated, studying Royal's eager face. He said, "You sure can. Keep Latigo off my back."

Poe had started to move away, but Johnny grabbed his arm and pulled him inside the saloon. He asked Latigo, "Was Rolly here when Trollinger came in?"

"He sure was," the bartender said. "Trying to work me for an eye opener like he does every morning."

"You're not going to believe a drunk like Poe, are you?" Roundtree demanded.

"Maybe," Johnny said. "Where were you when Trollinger came in, Rolly?"

Poe pointed at the bar. "I was standing next to the bar talking to Latigo. Like he said, I wanted a drink. I figured I had one coming after riding to hellangone twice to find Fremont, but Latigo was too stingy. He said he didn't owe me nothing and neither did Roundtree."

"What did Trollinger do?"

"I don't know," Poe said. "I didn't stay to find out. I seen him walk up to Charlie and hit him right in the snoot. He cracked him a good one. Charlie just kind o' bounced off the wall and went down. Then I lit a shuck out o' here 'cause I figgered there was gonna be shooting trouble. There was, too."

"That all you know?"

Poe held up his right hand. "I swear to God that's all. I didn't want no part o' the trouble, and I sure smelled trouble coming."

Johnny motioned toward the bat wings. "All right, Rolly. Git."

Poe wheeled and ran past Royal, who stood just inside the door, his eyes on Latigo. Johnny waited until the bat wings flapped shut behind Poe; then he turned slowly, knowing that the time had come when his life or death in line of duty would be decided. He thought briefly of Jan and wished this moment had not come, but it had, and there was no way he could avoid it.

"Roundtree, you're under arrest," Johnny said. "You, too, Moffat. Take off your gun belt and lay it on the table.

Don't make a fight out of it or I'll kill you. If I don't, Hawk Fremont will. You're both going to jail."

"What's the matter with you, Jones?" Roundtree cried shrilly. "You heard what we told you. It was self-defense. Trollinger came in here to kill me. What did you expect us to do?"

Johnny's right hand hovered over the butt of his gun, his gaze on Moffat. If Roundtree got into the fight, Johnny Jones would die. This was the gamble he had to take, that Roundtree would take a chance on a trial instead of shooting it out.

"I'm arresting you two men for the murder of Philip Fremont," Johnny said, "not for Vince—"

He never finished. He saw Moffat's lips pull back, saw the flash of his white teeth; and when he caught the slight dip of the gambler's right shoulder, he drew his gun. Two shots crashed out together; Johnny felt the breath of Moffat's bullet as it snapped past his face to smash a whisky bottle on a shelf behind him.

Moffat staggered, the big slug ripping into his chest. He dropped his gun and caught the edge of the poker table, but he could not keep his grip. His fingers slipped off the green surface and he collapsed, his head banging against the wall.

Johnny whirled to face Roundtree before Moffat fell, but the saloon man plainly wanted no part of a gun fight. His hands shot above his shoulders as he called, "No, no." Johnny kept him covered as he crossed to where Moffat lay and knelt beside him. He was dead.

Roundtree was halfway to the bat wings when Johnny rose. Dave Royal was holding his gun on Latigo, an exultant expression on his face.

"Get this fool out of here," Latigo said. "He looks like he wants to kill me."

"Why shouldn't I?" Royal demanded. "This camp has needed some funerals for years and it's finally getting them. Yours will help."

"Get him out, Jones," Latigo shouted. "He's kill-crazy."

"Come on, Dave," Johnny said. "Let's take Roundtree to jail."

They went out of the saloon, Roundtree in front, his hands in the air. Johnny and Royal were two steps behind him, their guns in their hands. The crowd broke away to let the three men through, then plunged into the saloon to see what had happened.

Five minutes later the door of Roundtree's cell slammed shut. Johnny locked it and said, "You and Al Lawler can talk your sins over," and stepped back into the sheriff's office.

Royal grinned at him. He said, "You've got it all cleaned up to hand over to Fremont when he gets here."

Johnny tried to grin back, but the grin wouldn't come. He took his bandanna out of his pocket and wiped his face, then he said, "Dave, did you stop to think what would have happened to you if Moffat had killed me?"

"I wasn't worried," Royal said. "I figured you'd take him."

"It was close," Johnny said. "Too close to be comfortable."

He hesitated, thinking it was unbelievable and irrational and a lot of other things. Dave Royal, a coward on Sunday morning, was the only man in Pulpit Rock who had the guts to back him all the way. He burst out, "Dave, I don't savvy. I just don't savvy."

Royal knew what he meant. He said gravely, "I don't, either, but I feel like a man who just got out of prison. I'll tell you one thing. It's a good feeling, a damned good feeling."

CHAPTER 29

As far as Johnny was concerned, his job was done. He had almost been killed trying to protect Phil and had failed. Even now, thinking back over the three days since Hawk Fremont had left town, he could not see anything he would have done differently. He had shot and killed or arrested the six men who had lynched Phil, with the exception of Clay Trollinger, who would either die in Doc Schuman's bed or recover to hang.

The only thing he had left to do was to turn his star over to Fremont and get Jan and ride out of town. He spent the rest of the morning packing the things in his cabin that he wanted, then went to the Bon Ton and made arrangements for Jake Norton to feed the prisoners. From there he walked to the stable, where he asked Jasper Hicks to pick up his possessions and anything Jan wanted to keep and haul them to the JJ. Hicks promised he would attend to the matter.

As Johnny turned to leave the stable, Hicks said, "Hawk Fremont's coming back this afternoon, ain't he?"

Johnny nodded. "That's when he said he'd be back."

Hicks cleared his throat uneasily. "And you're figuring on leaving?"

"You bet I am. As soon as I can give my star to Hawk."

"Johnny, maybe your mind's made up, but I'd like for you to think it over. I've talked to several men this morning, Jake Norton and Dave Royal and some others. We're all agreed we want you to stay. You're the kind of lawman we need. I don't know how we're gonna do it, but we've got to get rid of Fremont. He's run roughshod over us too long. We've had enough."

Johnny was pleased. In a way this balanced off what Charlie Roundtree had said about his being an innocent from the sagebrush. He shook his head. "I'm sorry. Jan and me have made up our minds."

It was noon when he left the livery stable. He didn't know if Jan was expecting him for dinner or not, but she could fix something for him if she wasn't. He didn't look for Fremont until the middle of the afternoon.

Jan had been watching for him. She ran out of the house to meet him and hugged him hard and cried a little, then asked, "It's over now, isn't it?"

"Sure is," he said. "I decided there wasn't any sense of us throwing good stuff away just because we're in a hurry to get out of this town, so I'm having Jasper Hicks haul my things to the JJ. As soon as we eat, you can pack your stuff, and he can fetch it too." He grinned. "That is, if you're going to feed me."

"I allowed I would," she said. "And I'm way ahead of you. I decided the same thing. Wherever we live, I'll need my sewing machine and most of the stuff I've collected since I came." She took his hand and led him inside.

150

"You were mad at me this morning for sending Dave Royal to Antoinette's place, weren't you?"

"It's all right," he said. "It turned out I needed him, but a wife—"

"I know," she said. "After this, I'll stay out of your affairs except for one more little thing. What will happen when Hawk Fremont gets here?"

"Nothing." He looked at her in surprise. "I'll give him the star and tell him to find a new deputy, and I'll walk out. Why?"

She shook her head. "I don't think it will work that way. If Hawk was an ordinary man, I guess it would, but Hawk isn't. He gets irrational when he's under pressure or gets upset. You know that as well as I do."

"Yeah, I know it," Johnny said, remembering Fremont's impatience over Zero Moran's failure to be at the Fremont house on time Saturday afternoon. "I don't savvy what you're getting at. Phil's dead and his killers have been taken care of. He's going to have to face it."

"He can't, Johnny," she said anxiously. "Don't you see? He can't. As far as I know, he never has faced his own failure, and that's what this is, so he'll have to have a scapegoat."

"You think that'll be me?"

"That's exactly what I think."

He considered it a moment, thinking that everything and everybody in Pulpit Rock had changed in the last three days. "I won't stand for being a scapegoat," he said.

"I just wanted to be sure you were thinking about it," she said. "Come on and eat. Dinner's ready."

As soon as they finished, he returned to the jail, hoping that Fremont would get back earlier in the afternoon than expected. He admitted to himself that Jan was right, that the news of Phil's death might turn Fremont into a raving maniac and that the trouble might not be over with after all.

He paced back and forth, his impatience growing as the minutes dragged by. Then at two o'clock he saw Dave Royal running across the courthouse yard toward the jail. From the expression on the banker's face, he guessed that Fremont was in town.

He stepped outside. When Royal reached him, he had

to wait for a time until he got his breath back, then he blurted, "Fremont's here. He rode in just now. He had Moran take the horses into the stable and he went into the Belle Union. Latigo will tell him what happened, only it won't be exactly the truth."

"He'll be along in about thirty seconds," Johnny said. "I'll wait inside. You'd better hike back to the bank."

Royal shook his head stubbornly. He was pale, a pulse was pounding in his temples, and the corners of his mouth were trembling. He was scared, Johnny saw, as scared as he had been Sunday morning, but there was a difference. He had not been man enough to stand up to his obligations then, but he was now.

"I'm staying, Johnny," he said, "unless you want me to go after Doc and the judge and Ed Allen. I can find more men if you think you'll need them. We've got to get rid of Fremont if we're going to make Pulpit Rock a decent place to live. This is the time to do it."

"All right, you can stay," Johnny said, "but don't go after anyone else. If Hawk's going to make trouble for me, it's my problem, not yours."

Royal swallowed with an effort. "Getting rid of him is our problem. You see, you don't know all you've done for this camp. Or for me. I'd rather die right here than to start running again. I think all of us feel that way. I guess you don't know what it is to be afraid, really afraid so you're all jelly deep down inside your belly, but I do, and I don't want to feel that way again, not ever."

Johnny nodded, thinking that he understood Dave Royal, but not at all sure that everybody else in Pulpit Rock felt that way. He said, "Here he comes."

CHAPTER 30

Johnny stood beside the desk and motioned for Dave Royal to move back against the wall. They were in that position when Fremont came in. He was dirty and tired, and his face was covered by stubble, but Johnny had seen him that way before. What he had not seen was the wild expression on the sheriff's face.

152

Johnny remembered thinking earlier in the afternoon that the news of Philip's death might turn Fremont into a raving maniac. Now, looking at the man, he sensed that that was exactly what had happened. The whisky he'd had in the Belle Union had made it worse.

Fremont stopped just inside the door. He was breathing hard, his fists doubled at his sides. Johnny said, "It's a sad occasion, Hawk. I'm sorry—"

"Don't tell me you're sorry, you stupid, bungling jackass," Fremont said as he took two long steps toward Johnny. "You incompetent son of a bitch. You let 'em murder Phil." He threw out a hand in an accusing gesture. "He was the only living relative I had, the only person on earth I loved."

Johnny was surprised that he used the word love. He said, "I did all I could. If anyone is a bungling fool, it's you. I sent Rolly Poe after you—"

Fremont was only a step away. Now he swung his right. Johnny saw it coming too late. He tried to snap his head back, tried to block the blow, but he had not expected it. Not this soon anyway. Fremont's punch caught him on the side of the head and knocked him back against the wall.

Johnny's feet slid out from under him and he went down, his head and back against the wall so he was supported in a sitting position. For a time he couldn't move or say anything. His head threatened to crack wide open. Even after he was able to speak and move, he remained motionless and silent, fully aware that to say or do the wrong thing would be an invitation for Fremont to kill him.

"Get on your feet, bucko," Fremont said. "I'm gonna give you a licking you'll never forget. I could forgive you for anything except letting them murder Phil. He was just a boy, a child. He never hurt nobody, but you sat here on your butt and let 'em kill him."

"You're dead wrong, Fremont," Royal said hoarsely. "We all did the best we could. Johnny was right when he said you were to blame for not coming back when Rolly Poe went after you."

Fremont whirled. He had not seen Royal. He laughed. "What's a pantywaist banker doing here? Get out of my office before I bust you into little pieces."

"No, you're the one getting out," Royal said. "You've buffaloed this camp long enough. Hand in your star and leave town. You don't have a friend in Pulpit Rock. You've got no call to blame Johnny when he almost got killed trying to save Phil."

"Me, turn in my star and get out?" Fremont grabbed Royal, who tried to hit him but swung wild. Fremont lifted him off his feet and threw him through the door as if he were a sack of grain. "Stay out, damn it. I hate to be bothered by a flea."

When Fremont turned, Johnny was on his feet. He hit the sheriff with a sledging, turning fist that crashed solidly against his jaw. Fremont sprawled backward on the floor. He shook his head and tried to get up, but he fell back, his head banging against a chair leg.

Royal charged back into the office and stopped, dumbfounded. "I'll be damned," he said. "I thought he'd knocked you silly."

"He just about did," Johnny said. "Let's get him up on that chair. If I have to pound some sense into him, I'll do it."

Together they lifted Fremont into one of the chairs. He was rubber-jointed, his head wobbling for a few seconds; then he came out of it. He stared at Johnny, who stood in front of him. He touched his jaw where he'd been hit, then he said as if he didn't believe it had actually happened, "You hit me."

"You're damned right I did," Johnny said. "Get something through your bone head. You don't have this camp treed the way you have for the last ten years. I've pulled the teeth of the tough bunch. If you'd done it a long time ago, Phil would be alive, but no, you had a good thing going."

"You listen to something else," Royal said. "The decent people of this camp have had all of you we want. If any of the tough outfit has any fight left, they'll tell you they're done paying you the graft you've been hauling in."

Suddenly Fremont began to cry. He tried to stop, but he couldn't. He bent forward, his great body shaking. It was a good three minutes before he could stop. When he did, he said, "Phil's dead." He started to cry again.

Johnny looked at Royal and Royal looked at Johnny, both having trouble believing what they were seeing.

There was something incongruous about Hawk Fremont weeping even in grief over his dead brother.

But Johnny had no compassion for this man, who so completely lacked compassion for others. He said, "I won't be a scapegoat for your negligence, Hawk. I've been waiting for you to get back so I could turn in my star. I've got just one thing to say. Six men took part in the lynching. I shot and killed three of them. Two are in jail. The sixth one, Clay Trollinger, is wounded. He's in Doc Schuman's house. Now it's up to you. Savvy?"

Fremont got out his bandanna and blew his nose. He said, "I savvy. Who's back there?" He jerked his head toward the cells.

"Al Lawler and Charlie Roundtree."

"How do you know they're the right ones?"

"Young Trollinger thought he was dying and made a statement. He named them."

Fremont gestured wearily. "All right. I'll take care of everything."

Johnny hesitated, not sure he should walk out and leave the sheriff's office in Fremont's hands. Oddly enough, he had thought he would have no feeling of responsibility once Fremont was back, but he found that he did.

The sheriff sat with his hands on his knees, his eyes fixed on something across the room. When he became aware that Johnny and Royal were still there, he motioned impatiently toward the door. "Go on. Go on. I told you I'd take care of everything."

Johnny jerked his head at Royal. They went outside, Johnny saying in a low tone, "I dunno, Dave. He's loco. I didn't think he would be this bad."

"We don't know what Latigo told him," Royal said, "but you're right. I never dreamed it would be this bad, either. I think he is really crazy."

"If there was anything that was decent in him," Johnny said thoughtfully, "it was focused on Phil. Now he's got nothing. When I hit him, I punctured a bubble of pride, I guess."

"We've got help coming," Royal said, nodding at Judge Herald and Doc Schuman and several other men who were crossing E Street on their way to the jail. "Let's see what they think. I know the judge wanted a showdown

155

with Fremont as soon as he got to town. Looks like this is the time."

A man screamed from inside the jail. Charlie Roundtree's voice, Johnny thought. As he wheeled around to face the door of the sheriff's office, he heard two shots. He started to run, hearing Royal gasp, "He's murdered them."

Fremont was coming out of the jail corridor just as Johnny reached the door of the office. Fremont said in a matter-of-fact voice, "I executed them for Phil's murder."

Johnny realized he had not taken off his star as he had intended. He knew, too, that he could not walk away and leave this situation to Royal and Herald and the others, that he was still a lawman and it was his responsibility to handle it.

"Hawk, put your gun on the desk," Johnny said. "I'm arresting you for the murder of Charlie Roundtree and Al Lawler."

"You?" Fremont said. "Arrest me?"

"That's right," Johnny said. "They were in jail to be tried. Nobody gave you the authority to execute them."

"This is my camp," Fremont said. "Nobody had to give me the authority. I had it." His strange, wild eyes narrowed, then he burst out, "Now I'm going to execute you, too, for negligence."

Fremont drew his gun, but Johnny had expected this. His .45 cleared leather and was leveled before Fremont had his gun completely lifted from the holster. Johnny fired; he saw the sheriff's massive body hammered back on his heels by the impact of the bullet, heard the roar of Fremont's shot as he pulled the trigger of his gun, the slug ripping into the floor of the office. Fremont found the strength to take one step forward as he tried to lift his gun, but he could not. He broke at knee and hip, and spilled forward on his face.

Johnny stepped out of the doorway to let Doc Schuman and the others through. He holstered his gun and raised his head to look at Pulpit Rock, which was supposed to fall sometime. Only a few days before, Hawk Fremont had been as solid as that huge rock, but he had come down as any human must who feels he is above the law.

The rock, Johnny thought, might be there for another hundred years.

When they surrounded him and offered their hands a moment later, he knew he wasn't leaving. By a baptism in blood he had become a part of this camp. He was needed, perhaps now more than ever.

He was not surprised when Ed Allen said, "Let me marry you and Jan today. Try to talk her into staying."

Dave Royal nodded. "Promise her something, John. My wife will never be ornery to her again. If she is, I'll belt her one."

"I'll talk to her," Johnny said. "We'll see."

As he walked away, he thought about Royal calling him John. It was the first time anyone in Pulpit Rock had called him that. He knew, then, that Dave Royal was not the only man who had changed in these last three days, that maturity comes in different ways to different men.

When he went into Jan's house, he saw that she had not started to pack. He said, "It's over now. Really over." He paused, wondering if he could find the right words to ask her to stay in Pulpit Rock.

She smiled and said, "You don't want to leave here, do you? They need you and maybe you need them."

"That's right," he said. "If I go back to the JJ, I'll be just another cowhand working for my dad. I don't think I can do it."

"I love you," she said softly. "If you go, I go, but if you stay, then I stay."

He kissed her, finding her lips sweet and rich with promise. The thought came to him that Mrs. Royal would break her neck to be friendly with Jan now. If she didn't, the chances were that Dave really would belt her one.

ABOUT THE AUTHOR

Born in Pomeroy, Washington, in 1906, Lee Leighton was educated in a one-room schoolhouse in the Willamette Valley. After graduating from the University of Oregon, he taught school for nineteen years, then devoted himself full-time to writing. The author of over 400 short stories and numerous novels under various pseudonyms, Lee Leighton has won three Spur Awards from the Western Writers of America.

The best
in modern fiction from
BALLANTINE